# COUNTRY CHRISTIE

# ALSO BY AGATHA CHRISTIE

★ novelized by Charles Osborne

AGATHA CHRISTIE

# COUNTRY CHRISTIE

TWELVE DEVONSHIRE MYSTERIES

HarperCollins*Publishers*

HarperCollins*Publishers* Ltd
1 London Bridge Street,
London SE1 9GF

www.harpercollins.co.uk

HarperCollins*Publishers*
Macken House, 39/40 Mayor Street Upper
Dublin 1, D01 C9W8, Ireland

First published by HarperCollins*Publishers* 2025
1

A catalogue record for this book is available from the British Library

ISBN: 978-0-00-873812-9

Set in Bembo Std by HarperCollins*Publishers* India

Printed and bound in the UK using 100%
Renewable Electricity by CPI Group (UK) Ltd

This book is produced from independently certified FSC™ paper
to ensure responsible forest management.

For more information visit: www.harpercollins.co.uk/green

# CONTENTS

# INTRODUCTION

# The Torquay Regatta

One of the great yearly events was the Torquay Regatta, which took place on the last Monday and Tuesday in August. I started saving up for it at the beginning of May. When I say I remember the Regatta I do not so much mean the yacht racing as the Fair which accompanied it. My sister Madge, of course, used to go with father to Haldon Pier to watch the sailing, and we usually had a house party staying for the Regatta Ball in the evening. Father, mother and Madge used to go to the Regatta Yacht Club tea in the afternoon, and all the various functions connected with sailing. Madge never did more sailing than she could help, because she was, throughout her life, an incurably bad sailor. However, a passionate interest was taken in our friends' yacht. There were picnics and parties, but this was the social side of the Regatta in which I was too young to participate.

My looked-forward-to joy in life was the Fair. The merry-go-rounds, where you rode on horses with manes, round and round and round, and a kind of switchback where you tore up and down slopes. Two machines blared music, and as you came round on the horses and the switchback cars, the tunes combined to make a horrible cacophony. Then there were all the shows—the Fat Woman; Madame Arensky, who told the Future; the Human Spider, horrible to look at; the Shooting Gallery, where Madge and my brother Monty spent always a great deal of time and money. And there were coconut shies, from which Monty used to obtain large quantities of coconuts and bring them home to me. I was passionately fond of coconut. I was given a few shies at the coconuts myself, gallantly allowed so far forward by the man in charge that I sometimes actually managed to knock a coconut off. Coconut shies were proper coconut shies then. Nowadays there are still shies, but the coconuts are so arranged in a kind of saucer that nothing but the most stupendous mixture of luck and strength would topple one. Then one had a sporting chance. Out of six shots you usually got one, and Monty once got five.

The hoop-las, the Kewpie dolls, the pointers and all those things had not arrived yet. There were various stalls that sold things. My particular passion was what were known as penny monkeys. They cost a penny, and they were fluffy little representations of monkeys on a long pin which you stuck into your coat. Every year I purchased six to eight of these, and added them to my collection—pink, green, brown, red, yellow. As the years went by it became more difficult to find a different colour or a different pattern.

There was also the famous nougat, which only appeared at the Fair. A man stood behind a table chopping nougat from an enormous pink and white block in front of him. He yelled, shouted, and offered bits for auction. 'Now, friends, sixpence for a stupendous piece! All right, love, cut it in half. Now then, what about that for fourpence?' and so on and so on. There were some ready-made packets which you could buy for twopence, but the fun was entering the auction. 'There, to the little lady there. Yes, twopence halfpenny to you.'

Goldfish did not arrive as a novelty in the Regatta until I was about twelve. It was a great excitement when they did. The whole stall was covered with goldfish bowls, one fish in each, and you threw ping-pong balls for them. If a ball lodged in the mouth of one of the bowls, the goldfish was yours. That, like the coconuts, was fairly easy to begin with. The first Regatta they appeared we got eleven between us, and bore them home in triumph to live in the Tub. But the price had soon advanced from a penny a ball to sixpence a ball.

In the evening there were fireworks. Since we could not see them from our house—or only the very high rockets—we usually spent the evening with some friends who lived just over the harbour. It was a nine o'clock party, with lemonade, ices and biscuits handed round. That was another delight of those days that I miss very much, not being of an alcoholic persuasion—the garden parties.

The garden parties of pre-1914 were something to be remembered. Everyone was dressed up to the nines, high-heeled shoes, muslin frocks with blue sashes, large leghorn hats with drooping roses. There were lovely ices—strawberry, vanilla, pistachio, orange-water and raspberry-water was the usual selection—with every kind of cream cake, of sandwich, of eclair, and peaches, muscat grapes, and nectarines. From this I deduce that garden parties were practically always held in August. I don't remember any strawberries and cream.

There was a certain pain in getting there, of course. Those who hadn't got carriages took a hired cab if they were aged or infirm, but all the young people walked a mile and a half to two miles from different parts of Torquay; some might be lucky and live near, but others were always bound to be a good way away, because Torquay is built on seven hills. There is no doubt that walking up hills in high-heeled shoes, holding up one's long skirt in one's left hand and one's parasol in the right, was something of an ordeal. It was worth it, however, to get to the garden party.

*Agatha Christie*

# The Plymouth Express

Alec Simpson, RN, stepped from the platform at Newton Abbot into a first-class compartment of the Plymouth Express. A porter followed him with a heavy suitcase. He was about to swing it up to the rack, but the young sailor stopped him.

'No—leave it on the seat. I'll put it up later. Here you are.'

'Thank you, sir.' The porter, generously tipped, withdrew.

Doors banged; a stentorian voice shouted: 'Plymouth only. Change for Torquay. Plymouth next stop.' Then a whistle blew, and the train drew slowly out of the station.

Lieutenant Simpson had the carriage to himself. The December air was chilly, and he pulled up the window. Then he sniffed vaguely, and frowned. What a smell there was! Reminded him of that time in hospital, and the operation on his leg. Yes, chloroform; that was it!

He let the window down again, changing his seat to one with its back to the engine. He pulled a pipe out of his pocket and lit it. For a little time he sat inactive, looking out into the night and smoking.

At last he roused himself, and opening the suitcase, took out some papers and magazines, then closed the suitcase again and endeavoured to shove it under the opposite seat—without success. Some obstacle resisted it. He shoved harder with rising impatience, but it still stuck out half-way into the carriage.

'Why the devil won't it go in?' he muttered, and hauling it out completely, he stooped down and peered under the seat ...

A moment later a cry rang out into the night, and the great train came to an unwilling halt in obedience to the imperative jerking of the communication cord.

'*Mon ami*,' said Poirot, 'you have, I know, been deeply interested in this mystery of the Plymouth Express. Read this.'

I picked up the note he flicked across the table to me. It was brief and to the point.

*Dear Sir,*
   *I shall be obliged if you will call upon me at your earliest convenience.*
   *Yours faithfully,*
   *Ebenezer Halliday*

The connection was not clear to my mind, and I looked inquiringly at Poirot.

For answer he took up the newspaper and read aloud: '"A sensational discovery was made last night. A young naval officer returning to Plymouth found under the seat of his compartment the body of a woman, stabbed through the heart. The officer at once pulled the communication cord, and the train was brought to a standstill. The woman, who was about thirty years of age, and richly dressed, has not yet been identified."

'And later we have this: "The woman found dead in the Plymouth Express has been identified as the Honourable Mrs Rupert Carrington." You see now, my friend? Or if you do not I will add this—Mrs Rupert Carrington was, before her marriage, Flossie Halliday, daughter of old man Halliday, the steel king of America.'

'And he has sent for you? Splendid!'

'I did him a little service in the past—an affair of bearer bonds. And once, when I was in Paris for a royal visit, I had Mademoiselle Flossie pointed out to me. *La jolie petite pensionnaire*! She had the *joli dot* too! It caused trouble. She nearly made a bad affair.'

'How was that?'

'A certain Count de la Rochefour. *Un bien mauvais sujet*! A bad hat, as you would say. An adventurer pure and simple, who knew how to appeal to a romantic young girl. Luckily her father got wind of it in time. He took her back to America in haste. I heard of her marriage some years later, but I know nothing of her husband.'

'H'm,' I said. 'The Honourable Rupert Carrington is no beauty, by all accounts. He'd pretty well run through his own money on the turf, and I should imagine old man Halliday's dollars came along in the nick of time. I should say that for a good-looking, well-mannered, utterly unscrupulous young scoundrel, it would be hard to find his match!'

'Ah, the poor little lady! *Elle n'est pas bien tombée*!'

'I fancy he made it pretty obvious at once that it was

her money, and not she, that had attacted him. I believe they drifted apart almost at once. I have heard rumours lately that there was to be a definite legal separation.'

'Old man Halliday is no fool. He would tie up her money pretty tight.'

'I dare say. Anyway, I know as a fact that the Honourable Rupert is said to be extremely hard up.'

'Aha! I wonder—'

'You wonder what?'

'My good friend, do not jump down my throat like that. You are interested, I see. Suppose you accompany me to see Mr Halliday. There is a taxi-stand at the corner.'

A few minutes sufficed to whirl us to the superb house in Park Lane rented by the American magnate. We were shown into the library, and almost immediately we were joined by a large stout man, with piercing eyes and an aggressive chin.

'M. Poirot?' said Mr Halliday. 'I guess I don't need to tell you what I want you for. You've read the papers, and I'm never one to let the grass grow under my feet. I happened to hear you were in London, and I remembered the good work you did over those bonds. Never forget a name. I've the pick of Scotland Yard, but I'll have my own man as well. Money no object. All the dollars were made for my little girl—and now she's gone, I'll spend my last cent to catch the damned scoundrel that did it! See? So it's up to you to deliver the goods.'

Poirot bowed.

'I accept, monsieur, all the more willingly that I saw your daughter in Paris several times. And now I will ask

4

you to tell me the circumstances of her journey to Plymouth and any other details that seem to you to bear upon the case.'

'Well, to begin with,' responded Halliday, 'she wasn't going to Plymouth. She was going to join a house-party at Avonmead Court, the Duchess of Swansea's place. She left London by the twelve-fourteen from Paddington, arriving at Bristol (where she had to change) at two-fifty. The principal Plymouth expresses, of course, run via Westbury, and do not go near Bristol at all. The twelve-fourteen does a non-stop run to Bristol, afterwards stopping at Weston, Taunton, Exeter and Newton Abbot. My daughter travelled alone in her carriage, which was reserved as far as Bristol, her maid being in a third class carriage in the next coach.'

Poirot nodded, and Mr Halliday went on: 'The party at Avonmead Court was to be a very gay one, with several balls, and in consequence my daughter had with her nearly all her jewels—amounting in value, perhaps, to about a hundred thousand dollars.'

'*Un moment*,' interrupted Poirot. 'Who had charge of the jewels? Your daughter, or the maid?'

'My daughter always took charge of them herself, carrying them in a small blue morocco case.'

'Continue, monsieur.'

'At Bristol the maid, Jane Mason, collected her mistress's dressing-bag and wraps, which were with her, and came to the door of Flossie's compartment. To her intense surprise, my daughter told her that she was not getting out at Bristol, but was going on farther. She directed Mason to get out the luggage and put it in the cloakroom. She could have tea in the refreshment-room, but she was to wait at the station for her mistress, who would return to Bristol by an up-train in the course of the afternoon. The maid, although very much astonished, did as she was told. She put the luggage in the cloakroom and had some tea. But up-train after up-train came in, and her mistress did not appear. After the arrival of the last train, she left the luggage where it was, and went to a hotel near the station for the night. This morning she read of the tragedy, and returned to town by the first available train.'

'Is there nothing to account for your daughter's sudden change of plan?'

'Well there is this: According to Jane Mason, at Bristol, Flossie was no longer alone in her carriage. There was a man in it who stood looking out of the farther window so that she could not see his face.'

'The train was a corridor one, of course?'

'Yes.'

'Which side was the corridor?'

'On the platform side. My daughter was standing in the corridor as she talked to Mason.'

'And there is no doubt in your mind—excuse me!' He got up, and carefully straightened the ink-stand which was a little askew. '*Je vous demande pardon*,' he continued, re-seating himself. 'It affects my nerves to see anything crooked. Strange, is it not? I was saying, monsieur, that there is no doubt in your mind as to this probably unexpected meeting being the cause of your daughter's sudden change of plan?'

'It seems the only reasonable supposition.'

'You have no idea as to who the gentleman in question might be?'

The millionaire hesitated for a moment, and then replied: 'No—I do not know at all.'

'Now—as to the discovery of the body?'

'It was discovered by a young naval officer who at once gave the alarm. There was a doctor on the train. He examined the body. She had been first chloroformed, and then stabbed. He gave it as his opinion that she had been dead about four hours, so it must have been done not long after leaving Bristol—probably between there and Weston, possibly between Weston and Taunton.'

'And the jewel-case?'

'The jewel-case, M. Poirot, was missing.'

'One thing more, monsieur. Your daughter's fortune—to whom does it pass at her death?'

'Flossie made a will soon after her marriage, leaving everything to her husband.' He hesitated for a minute, and then went on: 'I may as well tell you, Monsieur Poirot, that I regard my son-in-law as an unprincipled scoundrel, and that, by my advice, my daughter was on the eve of freeing herself from him by legal means—no difficult matter. I settled her money upon her in such a way that he could not touch it during her lifetime, but although they have lived entirely apart for some years, she had frequently acceded to his demands for money, rather than face an open scandal. However, I was determined to put an end to this. At last Flossie agreed, and my lawyers were instructed to take proceedings.'

'And where is Monsieur Carrington?'

'In town. I believe he was away in the country yesterday, but he returned last night.'

Poirot considered a little while. Then he said: 'I think that is all, monsieur.'

'You would like to see the maid, Jane Mason?'

'If you please.'

Halliday rang the bell, and gave a short order to the footman.

A few minutes later Jane Mason entered the room, a respectable, hard-featured woman, as emotionless in the face of tragedy as only a good servant can be.

'You will permit me to put a few questions? Your mistress, she was quite as usual before starting yesterday morning? Not excited or flurried?'

'Oh no, sir!'

'But at Bristol she was quite different?'

'Yes, sir, regular upset—so nervous she didn't seem to know what she was saying.'

'What did she say exactly?'

'Well, sir, as near as I can remember, she said: "Mason, I've got to alter my plans. Something has happened—I mean, I'm not getting out here after all. I must go on. Get out the luggage and put it in the cloakroom; then have some tea, and wait for me in the station."

'"Wait for you here, ma'am?" I asked.

'"Yes, yes. Don't leave the station. I shall return by a later train. I don't know when. It mayn't be until quite late."

'"Very well, ma'am," I says. It wasn't my place to ask questions, but I thought it very strange.'

'It was unlike your mistress, eh?'

'Very unlike her, sir.'

'What did you think?'

'Well, sir, I thought it was to do with the gentleman

8

in the carriage. She didn't speak to him, but she turned round once or twice as though to ask him if she was doing right.'

'But you didn't see the gentleman's face?'

'No, sir; he stood with his back to me all the time.'

'Can you describe him at all?'

'He had on a light fawn overcoat, and a travelling-cap. He was tall and slender, like and the back of his head was dark.'

'You didn't know him?'

'Oh no, I don't think so, sir.'

'It was not your master, Mr Carrington, by any chance?'

Mason looked rather startled.

'Oh, I don't think so, sir!'

'But you are not *sure*?'

'It was about the master's build, sir—but I never thought of it being him. We so seldom saw him... I couldn't say it *wasn't* him!'

Poirot picked up a pin from the carpet, and frowned at it severely; then he continued: 'Would it be possible for the man to have entered the train at Bristol before you reached the carriage?'

Mason considered.

'Yes, sir, I think it would. My compartment was very crowded, and it was some minutes before I could get out—and then there was a very large crowd on the platform, and that delayed me too. But he'd only have had a minute or two to speak to the mistress, that way. I took it for granted that he'd come along the corridor.'

'That is more probable, certainly.'

He paused, still frowning.

9

'You know how the mistress was dressed, sir?'

'The papers give a few details, but I would like you to confirm them.'

'She was wearing a white fox fur toque, sir, with a white spotted veil, and a blue frieze coat and skirt—the shade of blue they call electric.'

'H'm, rather striking.'

'Yes,' remarked Mr Halliday. 'Inspector Japp is in hopes that that may help us to fix the spot where the crime took place. Anyone who saw her would remember her.'

'*Précisément!*—Thank you, mademoiselle.' The maid left the room.

'Well!' Poirot got up briskly. 'That is all I can do here—except, monsieur, that I would ask you to tell me everything, but *everything*!'

'I have done so.'

'You are sure?'

'Absolutely.'

'Then there is nothing more to be said. I must decline the case.'

'Why?'

'Because you have not been frank with me.'

'I assure you—'

'No, you are keeping something back.'

There was a moment's pause, and then Halliday drew a paper from his pocket and handed it to my friend.

'I guess that's what you're after, Monsieur Poirot—though how you know about it fairly gets my goat!'

Poirot smiled, and unfolded the paper. It was a letter written in thin sloping handwriting. Poirot read it aloud.

*'Chère Madame,*

*It is with infinite pleasure that I look forward to the felicity of meeting you again. After your so amiable reply to my letter, I can hardly restrain my impatience. I have never forgotten those days in Paris. It is most cruel that you should be leaving London tomorrow. However, before very long, and perhaps sooner than you think, I shall have the joy of beholding once more the lady whose image has ever reigned supreme in my heart.*

*Believe, chère madame, all the assurances of my most devoted and unaltered sentiments—*

*Armand de la Rochefour.'*

Poirot handed the letter back to Halliday with a bow.

'I fancy, monsieur, that you did not know that your daughter intended renewing her acquaintance with the Count de la Rochefour?'

'It came as a thunderbolt to me! I found this letter in my daughter's handbag. As you probably know, Monsieur Poirot, this so-called count is an adventurer of the worst type.'

Poirot nodded.

'But I want to know how you knew of the existence of this letter?'

My friend smiled. 'Monsieur, I did not. But to track footmarks and recognize cigarette-ash is not sufficient for a detective. He must also be a good psychologist! I knew that you disliked and mistrusted your son-in-law. He benefits by your daughter's death; the maid's description of the mysterious man bears a sufficient resemblance to him. Yet you are not keen on his track! Why? Surely because your suspicions lie in another direction. Therefore you were keeping something back.'

'You're right, Monsieur Poirot. I was sure of Rupert's guilt until I found this letter. It unsettled me horribly.'

'Yes. The Count says "Before very long, and perhaps sooner than you think." Obviously he would not want to wait until you should get wind of his reappearance. Was it he who travelled down from London by the twelve-fourteen, and came along the corridor to your daughter's compartment? The Count de la Rochefour is also, if I remember rightly, tall and dark!'

The millionaire nodded.

'Well, monsieur, I will wish you good day. Scotland Yard has, I presume, a list of the jewels?'

'Yes, I believe Inspector Japp is here now if you would like to see him.'

Japp was an old friend of ours, and greeted Poirot with a sort of affectionate contempt.

'And how are you, monsieur? No bad feeling between us, though we *have* got our different ways of looking at things. How are the "little grey cells", eh? Going strong?'

Poirot beamed upon him. 'They function, my good Japp; assuredly they do!'

'Then that's all right. Think it was the Honourable Rupert, or a crook? We're keeping an eye on all the regular places, of course. We shall know if the shiners are disposed of, and of course whoever did it isn't going to keep them to admire their sparkle. Not likely! I'm trying to find out where Rupert Carrington was yesterday. Seems a bit of a mystery about it. I've got a man watching him.'

'A great precaution, but perhaps a day late,' suggested Poirot gently.

'You always will have your joke, Monsieur Poirot. Well, I'm off to Paddington. Bristol, Weston, Taunton, that's my beat. So long.'

'You will come round and see me this evening, and tell me the result?'

'Sure thing, if I'm back.'

'The good inspector believes in matter in motion,' murmured Poirot as our friend departed. 'He travels; he measures footprints; he collects mud and cigarette-ash! He is extremely busy! He is zealous beyond words! And if I mentioned psychology to him, do you know what he would do, my friend? He would smile! He would say to himself: "Poor old Poirot! He ages! He grows senile!" Japp is the "younger generation knocking on the door." And *ma foi*! They are so busy knocking that they do not notice that the door is open!'

'And what are you going to do?'

'As we have *carte blanche*, I shall expend threepence in ringing up the Ritz—where you may have noticed our Count is staying. After that, as my feet are a little damp, and I have sneezed twice, I shall return to my rooms and make myself a *tisane* over the spirit lamp!'

I did not see Poirot again until the following morning. I found him placidly finishing his breakfast.

'Well?' I inquired eagerly. 'What has happened?'

'Nothing.'

'But Japp?'

'I have not seen him.'

'The Count?'

'He left the Ritz the day before yesterday.'

'The day of the murder?'

13

'Yes.'

'Then that settles it! Rupert Carrington is cleared.'

'Because the Count de la Rochefour has left the Ritz? You go too fast, my friend.'

'Anyway, he must be followed, arrested! But what could be his motive?'

'One hundred thousand dollars' worth of jewellery is a very good motive for anyone. No, the question to my mind is: why kill her? Why not simply steal the jewels? She would not prosecute.'

'Why not?'

'Because she is a woman, *mon ami*. She once loved this man. Therefore she would suffer her loss in silence. And the Count, who is an extremely good psychologist where women are concerned—hence his successes— would know that perfectly well! On the other hand, if Rupert Carrington killed her, why take the jewels which would incriminate him fatally?'

'As a blind.'

'Perhaps you are right, my friend. Ah, here is Japp! I recognize his knock.'

The inspector was beaming good-humouredly.

'Morning, Poirot. Only just got back. I've done some good work! And you?'

'Me, I have arranged my ideas,' replied Poirot placidly.

Japp laughed heartily.

'Old chap's getting on in years,' he observed beneath his breath to me. 'That won't do for us young folk,' he said aloud.

'*Quel dommage?*' Poirot inquired.

'Well, do you want to hear what I've done?'

'You permit me to make a guess? You have found the

knife with which the crime was committed, by the side of the line between Weston and Taunton, and you have interviewed the paper-boy who spoke to Mrs Carrington at Weston!'

Japp's jaw fell. 'How on earth did you know? Don't tell me it was those almighty "little grey cells" of yours!'

'I am glad you admit for once that they are *all mighty*! Tell me, did she give the paper-boy a shilling for himself?'

'No, it was half a crown!' Japp had recovered his temper, and grinned. 'Pretty extravagant, these rich Americans!'

'And in consequence the boy did not forget her?'

'Not he. Half-crowns don't come his way every day. She hailed him and bought two magazines. One had a picture of a girl in blue on the cover. "That'll match me," she said. Oh, he remembered her perfectly. Well, that was enough for me. By the doctor's evidence, the crime *must* have been committed before Taunton. I guessed they'd throw the knife away at once, and I walked down the line looking for it; and sure enough, there it was. I made inquiries at Taunton about our man, but of course it's a big station, and it wasn't likely they'd notice him. He probably got back to London by a later train.'

Poirot nodded. 'Very likely.'

'But I found another bit of news when I got back. They're passing the jewels, all right! That large emerald was pawned last night—by one of the regular lot. Who do you think it was?'

'I don't know—except that he was a short man.'

Japp stared. 'Well, you're right there. He's short enough. It was Red Narky.'

'Who is Red Narky?' I asked.

'A particularly sharp jewel-thief, sir. And not one to stick at murder. Usually works with a woman—Gracie Kidd; but she doesn't seem to be in it this time—unless she's got off to Holland with the rest of the swag.'

'You've arrested Narky?'

'Sure thing. But mind you, it's the other man we want—the man who went down with Mrs Carrington in the train. He was the one who planned the job, right enough. But Narky won't squeal on a pal.'

I noticed Poirot's eyes had become very green.

'I think,' he said gently, 'that I can find Narky's pal for you, all right.'

'One of your little ideas, eh?' Japp eyed Poirot sharply. 'Wonderful how you manage to deliver the goods sometimes, at your age and all. Devil's own luck, of course.'

'Perhaps, perhaps,' murmured my friend. 'Hastings, my hat. And the brush. So! My galoshes, if it still rains! We must not undo the good work of that *tisane*. *Au revoir*, Japp!'

'Good luck to you, Poirot.'

Poirot hailed the first taxi we met, and directed the driver to Park Lane.

When we drew up before Halliday's house, he skipped out nimbly, paid the driver and rang the bell. To the footman who opened the door he made a request in a low voice, and we were immediately taken upstairs. We went up to the top of the house, and were shown into a small neat bedroom.

Poirot's eyes roved round the room and fastened themselves on a small black trunk. He knelt in front of

16

it, scrutinized the labels on it, and took a small twist of wire from his pocket.

'Ask Mr Halliday if he will be so kind as to mount to me here,' he said over his shoulder to the footman.

The man departed, and Poirot gently coaxed the lock of the trunk with a practised hand. In a few minutes the lock gave, and he raised the lid of the trunk. Swiftly he began rummaging among the clothes it contained, flinging them out on the floor.

There was a heavy step on the stairs, and Halliday entered the room.

'What in hell are you doing here?' he demanded, staring.

'I was looking, monsieur, for *this*.' Poirot withdrew from the trunk a coat and skirt of bright blue frieze, and a small toque of white fox fur.

'What are you doing with my trunk?' I turned to see that the maid, Jane Mason, had entered the room.

'If you will just shut the door, Hastings. Thank you. Yes, and stand with your back against it. Now, Mr Halliday, let me introduce you to Gracie Kidd, otherwise Jane Mason, who will shortly rejoin her accomplice, Red Narky, under the kind escort of Inspector Japp.'

Poirot waved a deprecating hand. 'It was of the most simple!' He helped himself to more caviar.

'It was the maid's insistence on the clothes that her mistress was wearing that first struck me. Why was she so anxious that our attention should be directed to them? I reflected that we had only the maid's word for the mysterious man in the carriage at Bristol. As far as the doctor's evidence went, Mrs Carrington might

17

easily have been murdered *before* reaching Bristol. But if so, then the maid must be an accomplice. And if she were an accomplice, she would not wish this point to rest on her evidence alone. The clothes Mrs Carrington was wearing were of a striking nature. A maid usually has a good deal of choice as to what her mistress shall wear. Now if, after Bristol, anyone saw a lady in a bright blue coat and skirt, and a fur toque, he will be quite ready to swear he had seen Mrs Carrington.

'I began to reconstruct. The maid would provide herself with duplicate clothes. She and her accomplice chloroform and stab Mrs Carrington between London and Bristol, probably taking advantage of a tunnel. Her body is rolled under the seat; and the maid takes her place. At Weston she must make herself noticed. How? In all probability, a newspaperboy will be selected. She will insure his remembering her by giving him a large tip. She also drew his attention to the colour of her dress by a remark about one of the magazines. After leaving Weston, she throws the knife out of the window to mark the place where the crime presumably occurred, and changes her clothes, or buttons a long mackintosh over them. At Taunton she leaves the train and returns to Bristol as soon as possible, where her accomplice has duly left the luggage in the cloakroom. He hands over the ticket and himself returns to London. She waits on the platform, carrying out her role, goes to a hotel for the night and returns to town in the morning, exactly as she said.

'When Japp returned from his expedition, he confirmed all my deductions. He also told me that a well-known crook was passing the jewels. I knew that whoever it was would be the exact opposite of the man Jane Mason described. When I heard that it was Red Narky, who always worked with Gracie Kidd—well, I knew just where to find her.'

'And the Count?'

'The more I thought of it, the more I was convinced that he had nothing to do with it. That gentleman is much too careful of his own skin to risk murder. It would be out of keeping with his character.'

'Well, Monsieur Poirot,' said Halliday, 'I owe you a big debt. And the cheque I write after lunch won't go near to settling it.'

Poirot smiled modestly, and murmured to me: 'The good Japp, he shall get the official credit, all right, but though he has got his Gracie Kidd, I think that I, as the Americans say, have got his goat!'

# The Unbreakable Alibi

Tommy and Tuppence were busy sorting correspondence. Tuppence gave an exclamation and handed a letter across to Tommy.

'A new client,' she said importantly.

'Ha!' said Tommy. 'What do we deduce from this letter, Watson? Nothing much, except the somewhat obvious fact that Mr—er—Montgomery Jones is not one of the world's best spellers, thereby proving that he has been expensively educated.'

'Montgomery Jones?' said Tuppence. 'Now what do I know about a Montgomery Jones? Oh, yes, I have got it now. I think Janet St Vincent mentioned him. His mother was Lady Aileen Montgomery, very crusty and high church, with gold crosses and things, and she married a man called Jones who is immensely rich.'

'In fact the same old story,' said Tommy. 'Let me see, what time does this Mr M. J. wish to see us? Ah, eleven-thirty.'

At eleven-thirty precisely, a very tall young man with an amiable and ingenuous countenance entered the outer office and addressed himself to Albert, the office boy.

'Look here—I say. Can I see Mr—er—Blunt?'

'Have you an appointment, sir?' said Albert.

'I don't quite know. Yes, I suppose I have. What I mean is, I wrote a letter—'

'What name, sir?'

'Mr Montgomery Jones.'

'I will take your name in to Mr Blunt.'

He returned after a brief interval.

'Will you wait a few minutes please, sir. Mr Blunt is engaged on a very important conference at present.'

'Oh—er—yes—certainly,' said Mr Montgomery Jones.

Having, he hoped, impressed his client sufficiently Tommy rang the buzzer on his desk, and Mr Montgomery Jones was ushered into the inner office by Albert.

Tommy rose to greet him, and shaking him warmly by the hand motioned towards the vacant chair.

'Now, Mr Montgomery Jones,' he said briskly. 'What can we have the pleasure of doing for you?'

Mr Montgomery Jones looked uncertainly at the third occupant of the office.

'My confidential secretary, Miss Robinson,' said Tommy. 'You can speak quite freely before her. I take it that this is some family matter of a delicate kind?'

'Well—not exactly,' said Mr Montgomery Jones.

'You surprise me,' said Tommy. 'You are not in trouble of any kind yourself, I hope?'

'Oh, rather not,' said Mr Montgomery Jones.

'Well,' said Tommy, 'perhaps you will—er—state the facts plainly.'

That, however, seemed to be the one thing that Mr Montgomery Jones could not do.

'It's a dashed odd sort of thing I have got to ask you,' he said hesitatingly. 'I—er—I really don't know how to set about it.'

'We never touch divorce cases,' said Tommy.

'Oh Lord, no,' said Mr Montgomery Jones. 'I don't mean that. It is just, well—it's a deuced silly sort of a joke. That's all.'

'Someone has played a practical joke on you of a mysterious nature?' suggested Tommy.

But Mr Montgomery Jones once more shook his head.

'Well,' said Tommy, retiring gracefully from the position, 'take your own time and let us have it in your own words.'

There was a pause.

'You see,' said Mr Jones at last, 'it was at dinner. I sat next to a girl.'

'Yes?' said Tommy encouragingly.

'She was a—oh well, I really can't describe her, but she was simply one of the most sporting girls I ever met. She's an Australian, over here with another girl, sharing a flat with her in Clarges Street. She's simply game for anything. I absolutely can't tell you the effect that girl had on me.'

'We can quite imagine it, Mr Jones,' said Tuppence.

She saw clearly that if Mr Montgomery Jones's troubles were ever to be extracted a sympathetic feminine touch was needed, as distinct from the businesslike methods of Mr Blunt.

'We can understand,' said Tuppence encouragingly.

'Well, the whole thing came as an absolute shock to me,' said Mr Montgomery Jones, 'that a girl could well—knock you over like that. There had been another girl—in fact two other girls. One was awfully jolly and all that, but I didn't much like her chin. She danced marvellously though, and I have known her all my life, which makes a fellow feel kind of safe, you know. And then there was one of the girls at the "Frivolity." Frightfully amusing, but of course there would be a lot of ructions with the matter over that, and anyway I didn't really want to marry either of them, but I was thinking about things, you know, and then—slap out of the blue—I sat next to this girl and—'

'The whole world was changed,' said Tuppence in a feeling voice.

Tommy moved impatiently in his chair. He was by now somewhat bored by the recital of Mr Montgomery Jones's love affairs.

'You put it awfully well,' said Mr Montgomery Jones. 'That is absolutely what it was like. Only, you know, I fancy she didn't think much of me. You mayn't think it, but I am not terribly clever.'

'Oh, you mustn't be too modest,' said Tuppence.

'Oh, I do realise that I am not much of a chap,' said Mr Jones with an engaging smile. 'Not for a perfectly marvellous girl like that. That is why I just feel I have got to put this thing through. It's my only chance. She's such a sporting girl that she would never go back on her word.'

'Well, I am sure we wish you luck and all that,' said Tuppence kindly. 'But I don't exactly see what you want us to do.'

'Oh Lord,' said Mr Montgomery Jones. 'Haven't I explained?'

'No,' said Tommy, 'you haven't.'

'Well, it was like this. We were talking about detective stories. Una—that's her name—is just as keen about them as I am. We got talking about one in particular. It all hinges on an alibi. Then we got talking about alibis and faking them. Then I said—no, she said—now which of us was it that said it?'

'Never mind which of you it was,' said Tuppence.

'I said it would be a jolly difficult thing to do. She disagreed—said it only wanted a bit of brain work. We got all hot and excited about it and in the end she said, "I will make you a sporting offer. What do you bet that I can produce an alibi that nobody can shake?"'

'"Anything you like," I said, and we settled it then and there. She was frightfully cocksure about the whole thing. "It's an odds on chance for me," she said. "Don't be so sure of that," I said. "Supposing you lose and I ask you for anything I like?" She laughed and said she came of a gambling family and I could.'

'Well?' said Tuppence as Mr Jones came to a pause and looked at her appealingly.

'Well, don't you see? It is up to me. It is the only chance I have got of getting a girl like that to look at me. You have no idea how sporting she is. Last summer she was out in a boat and someone bet her she wouldn't jump overboard and swim ashore in her clothes, and she did it.'

'It is a very curious proposition,' said Tommy. 'I am not quite sure I yet understand it.'

'It is perfectly simple,' said Mr Montgomery Jones. 'You must be doing this sort of thing all the time. Investigating fake alibis and seeing where they fall down.'

24

'Oh—er—yes, of course,' said Tommy. 'We do a lot of that sort of work.'

'Someone has got to do it for me,' said Montgomery Jones. 'I shouldn't be any good at that sort of thing myself. You have only got to catch her out and everything is all right. I dare say it seems rather a futile business to you, but it means a lot to me and I am prepared to pay—er—all necessary whatnots, you know.'

'That will be all right,' said Tuppence. 'I am sure Mr Blunt will take this case on for you.'

'Certainly, certainly,' said Tommy. 'A most refreshing case, most refreshing indeed.'

Mr Montgomery Jones heaved a sigh of relief, pulled a mass of papers from his pocket and selected one of them. 'Here it is,' he said. 'She says, "I am sending you proof I was in two distinct places at one and the same time. According to one story I dined at the Bon Temps Restaurant in Soho by myself, went to the Duke's Theatre and had supper with a friend, Mr le Marchant, at the Savoy—*but* I was also staying at the Castle Hotel, Torquay, and only returned to London on the following morning. You have got to find out which of the two stories is the true one and how I managed the other."'

'There,' said Mr Montgomery Jones. 'Now you see what it is that I want you to do.'

'A most refreshing little problem,' said Tommy. 'Very naive.'

'Here is Una's photograph,' said Mr Montgomery Jones. 'You will want that.'

'What is the lady's full name?' inquired Tommy.

'Miss Una Drake. And her address is 180 Clarges Street.'

'Thank you,' said Tommy. 'Well, we will look into the matter for you, Mr Montgomery Jones. I hope we shall have good news for you very shortly.'

'I say, you know, I am no end grateful,' said Mr Jones, rising to his feet and shaking Tommy by the hand. 'It has taken an awful load off my mind.'

Having seen his client out, Tommy returned to the inner office. Tuppence was at the cupboard that contained the classic library.

'Inspector French,' said Tuppence.

'Eh?' said Tommy.

'Inspector French, of course,' said Tuppence. 'He always does alibis. I know the exact procedure. We have to go over everything and check it. At first it will seem all right and then when we examine it more closely we shall find the flaw.'

'There ought not to be much difficulty about that,' agreed Tommy. 'I mean, knowing that one of them is a fake to start with makes the thing almost a certainty, I should say. That is what worries me.'

'I don't see anything to worry about in that.'

'I am worrying about the girl,' said Tommy. 'She will probably be let in to marry that young man whether she wants to or not.'

'Darling,' said Tuppence, 'don't be foolish. Women are never the wild gamblers they appear. Unless that girl was already perfectly prepared to marry that pleasant, but rather empty-headed young man, she would never have let herself in for a wager of this kind. But, Tommy, believe me, she will marry him with more enthusiasm and respect if he wins the wager than if she has to make it easy for him some other way.'

'You do think you know about everything,' said her husband.

'I do,' said Tuppence.

'And now to examine our data,' said Tommy, drawing the papers towards him. 'First the photograph—h'm—quite a nice looking girl—and quite a good photograph, I should say. Clear and easily recognisable.'

'We must get some other girls' photographs,' said Tuppence.

'Why?'

'They always do,' said Tuppence. 'You show four or five to waiters and they pick out the right one.'

'Do you think they do?' said Tommy—'pick out the right one, I mean.'

'Well, they do in books,' said Tuppence.

'It is a pity that real life is so different from fiction,' said Tommy. 'Now then, what have we here? Yes, this is the London lot. Dined at the Bon Temps seven-thirty. Went to Duke's Theatre and saw *Delphiniums Blue*. Counterfoil of theatre ticket enclosed. Supper at the Savoy with Mr le Marchant. We can, I suppose, interview Mr le Marchant.'

'That tells us nothing at all,' said Tuppence, 'because if he is helping her to do it he naturally won't give the show away. We can wash out anything he says now.'

'Well, here is the Torquay end,' went on Tommy. 'Twelve o'clock from Paddington, had lunch in the Restaurant Car, receipted bill enclosed. Stayed at Castle Hotel for one night. Again receipted bill.'

'I think this is all rather weak,' said Tuppence. 'Anyone can buy a theatre ticket, you need never go near the theatre. The girl just went to Torquay and the London thing is a fake.'

'If so, it is rather a sitter for us,' said Tommy. 'Well, I suppose we might as well go and interview Mr le Marchant.'

Mr le Marchant proved to be a breezy youth who betrayed no great surprise on seeing them.

'Una has got some little game on, hasn't she?' he asked. 'You never know what that kid is up to.'

'I understand, Mr le Marchant,' said Tommy, 'that Miss Drake had supper with you at the Savoy last Tuesday evening.'

'That's right,' said Mr le Marchant, 'I know it was Tuesday because Una impressed it on me at the time and what's more she made me write it down in a little book.'

With some pride he showed an entry faintly pencilled. 'Having supper with Una. Savoy. Tuesday 19th.'

'Where had Miss Drake been earlier in the evening? Do you know?'

'She had been to some rotten show called *Pink Peonies* or something like that. Absolute slosh, so she told me.'

'You are quite sure Miss Drake was with you that evening?'

Mr le Marchant stared at him.

'Why, of course. Haven't I been telling you?'

'Perhaps she asked you to tell us,' said Tuppence.

'Well, for a matter of fact she did say something that was rather dashed odd. She said—what was it now? "You think you are sitting here having supper with me, Jimmy, but really I am having supper two hundred miles away in Devonshire." Now that was a dashed odd thing to say, don't you think so? Sort of astral body stuff. The funny thing is that a pal of mine, Dicky Rice, thought he saw her there.'

28

'Who is this Mr Rice?'

'Oh, just a friend of mine. He had been down in Torquay staying with an aunt. Sort of old bean who is always going to die and never does. Dicky had been down doing the dutiful nephew. He said, "I saw that Australian girl one day—Una something or other. Wanted to go and talk to her, but my aunt carried me off to chat with an old dear in a bath chair." I said: "When was this?" and he said, "Oh, Tuesday about tea time." I told him, of course, that he had made a mistake, but it was odd, wasn't it? With Una saying that about Devonshire that evening?'

'Very odd,' said Tommy. 'Tell me, Mr le Marchant, did anyone you know have supper near you at the Savoy?'

'Some people called Oglander were at the next table.'

'Do they know Miss Drake?'

'Oh yes, they know her. They are not frightful friends or anything of that kind.'

'Well, if there's nothing more you can tell us, Mr le Marchant, I think we will wish you good-morning.'

'Either that chap is an extraordinarily good liar,' said Tommy as they reached the street, 'or else he is speaking the truth.'

'Yes,' said Tuppence, 'I have changed my opinion. I have a sort of feeling now that Una Drake was at the Savoy for supper that night.'

'We will now go to the Bon Temps,' said Tommy. 'A little food for starving sleuths is clearly indicated. Let's just get a few girls' photographs first.'

This proved rather more difficult than was expected. Turning into a photographers and demanding a few assorted photographs, they were met with a cold rebuff.

'Why are all the things that are so easy and simple in books so difficult in real life,' wailed Tuppence. 'How horribly suspicious they looked. What do you think they thought we wanted to do with the photographs? We had better go and raid Jane's flat.'

Tuppence's friend Jane proved of an accommodating disposition and permitted Tuppence to rummage in a drawer and select four specimens of former friends of Jane's who had been shoved hastily in to be out of sight and mind.

Armed with this galaxy of feminine beauty they proceeded to the Bon Temps where fresh difficulties and much expense awaited them. Tommy had to get hold of each waiter in turn, tip him and then produce the assorted photographs. The result was unsatisfactory. At least three of the photographs were promising starters as having dined there last Tuesday. They then returned to the office where Tuppence immersed herself in an A.B.C.

'Paddington twelve o'clock. Torquay three thirty-five. That's the train and le Marchant's friend, Mr Sago or Tapioca or something saw her there about tea time.'

'We haven't checked his statement, remember,' said Tommy. 'If, as you said to begin with, le Marchant is a friend of Una Drake's he may have invented this story.'

'Oh, we'll hunt up Mr Rice,' said Tuppence. 'I have a kind of hunch that Mr le Marchant was speaking the truth. No, what I am trying to get at now is this. Una Drake leaves London by the twelve o'clock train, possibly takes a room at a hotel and unpacks. Then she takes a train back to town arriving in time to get to the

Savoy. There is one at four-forty gets up to Paddington at nine-ten.'

'And then?' said Tommy.

'And then,' said Tuppence frowning, 'it is rather more difficult. There is a midnight train from Paddington down again, but she could hardly take that, that would be too early.'

'A fast car,' suggested Tommy.

'H'm,' said Tuppence. 'It is just on two hundred miles.'

'Australians, I have always been told, drive very recklessly.'

'Oh, I suppose it could be done,' said Tuppence. 'She would arrive there about seven.'

'Are you supposing her to have nipped into her bed at the Castle Hotel without being seen? Or arriving there explaining that she had been out all night and could she have her bill, please?'

'Tommy,' said Tuppence, 'we are idiots. She needn't have gone back to Torquay at all. She has only got to get a friend to go to the hotel there and collect her luggage and pay her bill. Then you get the receipted bill with the proper date on it.'

'I think on the whole we have worked out a very sound hypothesis,' said Tommy. 'The next thing to do is to catch the twelve o'clock train to Torquay tomorrow and verify our brilliant conclusions.'

Armed with a portfolio of photographs, Tommy and Tuppence duly established themselves in a first-class carriage the following morning, and booked seats for the second lunch.

'It probably won't be the same dining car attendants,'

said Tommy. 'That would be too much luck to expect. I expect we shall have to travel up and down to Torquay for days before we strike the right ones.'

'This alibi business is very trying,' said Tuppence. 'In books it is all passed over in two or three paragraphs. Inspector Something then boarded the train to Torquay and questioned the dining car attendants and so ended the story.'

For once, however, the young couple's luck was in. In answer to their question the attendant who brought their bill for lunch proved to be the same one who had been on duty the preceding Tuesday. What Tommy called the ten-shilling touch then came into action and Tuppence produced the portfolio.

'I want to know,' said Tommy, 'if any of these ladies had lunch on this train on Tuesday last?'

In a gratifying manner worthy of the best detective fiction the man at once indicated the photograph of Una Drake.

'Yes, sir, I remember that lady, and I remember that it was Tuesday, because the lady herself drew attention to the fact, saying it was always the luckiest day in the week for her.'

'So far, so good,' said Tuppence as they returned to their compartment. 'And we will probably find that she booked at the hotel all right. It is going to be more difficult to prove that she travelled back to London, but perhaps one of the porters at the station may remember.'

Here, however, they drew a blank, and crossing to the up platform Tommy made inquiries of the ticket collector and of various porters. After the distribution of half-crowns as a preliminary to inquiring, two of the porters picked out one of the other photographs with a vague remembrance that someone like that travelled to town by the four-forty that afternoon, but there was no identification of Una Drake.

'But that doesn't prove anything,' said Tuppence as they left the station. 'She may have travelled by that train and no one noticed her.'

'She may have gone from the other station, from Torre.'

'That's quite likely,' said Tuppence, 'however, we can see to that after we have been to the hotel.'

The Castle Hotel was a big one overlooking the sea. After booking a room for the night and signing the register, Tommy observed pleasantly.

'I believe you had a friend of ours staying here last Tuesday. Miss Una Drake.'

The young lady in the bureau beamed at him.

'Oh, yes, I remember quite well. An Australian young lady, I believe.'

At a sign from Tommy, Tuppence produced the photograph.

'That is rather a charming photograph of her, isn't it?' said Tuppence.

'Oh, very nice, very nice indeed, quite stylish.'

'Did she stay here long?' inquired Tommy.

'Only the one night. She went away by the express the next morning back to London. It seemed a long way to come for one night, but of course I suppose Australian ladies don't think anything of travelling.'

'She is a very sporting girl,' said Tommy, 'always having adventures. It wasn't here, was it, that she went out to dine with some friends, went for a drive in their car afterwards, ran the car into a ditch and wasn't able to get home till morning?'

'Oh, no,' said the young lady. 'Miss Drake had dinner here in the hotel.'

'Really,' said Tommy, 'are you sure of that? I mean—how do you know?'

'Oh, I saw her.'

'I asked because I understood she was dining with some friends in Torquay,' explained Tommy.

'Oh, no, sir, she dined here.' The young lady laughed and blushed a little. 'I remember she had on a most sweetly pretty frock. One of those new flowered chiffons all over pansies.'

'Tuppence, this tears it,' said Tommy when they had been shown upstairs to their room.

'It does rather,' said Tuppence. 'Of course that woman may be mistaken. We will ask the waiter at dinner. There can't be very many people here just at this time of year.'

This time it was Tuppence who opened the attack.

'Can you tell me if a friend of mine was here last Tuesday?' she asked the waiter with an engaging smile. 'A Miss Drake, wearing a frock all over pansies, I believe.' She produced a photograph. 'This lady.'

The waiter broke into immediate smiles of recognition.

'Yes, yes, Miss Drake, I remember her very well. She told me she came from Australia.'

'She dined here?'

'Yes. It was last Tuesday. She asked me if there was anything to do afterwards in the town.'

'Yes?'

'I told her the theatre, the Pavilion, but in the end she

34

decided not to go and she stayed here listening to our orchestra.'

'Oh, damn!' said Tommy, under his breath.

'You don't remember what time she had dinner, do you?' asked Tuppence.

'She came down a little late. It must have been about eight o'clock.'

'Damn, Blast, and Curse,' said Tuppence as she and Tommy left the dining-room. 'Tommy, this is all going wrong. It seemed so clear and lovely.'

'Well, I suppose we ought to have known it wouldn't all be plain sailing.'

'Is there any train she could have taken after that, I wonder?'

'Not one that would have landed her in London in time to go to the Savoy.'

'Well,' said Tuppence, 'as a last hope I am going to talk to the chambermaid. Una Drake had a room on the same floor as ours.'

The chambermaid was a voluble and informative woman. Yes, she remembered the young lady quite well. That was her picture right enough. A very nice young lady, very merry and talkative. Had told her a lot about Australia and the kangaroos.

The young lady rang the bell about half-past nine and asked for her bottle to be filled and put in her bed, and also to be called the next morning at half-past seven—with coffee instead of tea.

'You did call her and she was in her bed?' asked Tuppence.

'Why, yes, Ma'am, of course.'

'Oh, I only wondered if she was doing exercises or

anything,' said Tuppence wildly. 'So many people do in the early morning.'

'Well, that seems cast-iron enough,' said Tommy when the chambermaid had departed. 'There is only one conclusion to be drawn from it. It is the London side of the thing that *must* be faked.'

'Mr le Marchant must be a more accomplished liar than we thought,' said Tuppence.

'We have a way of checking his statements,' said Tommy. 'He said there were people sitting at the next table whom Una knew slightly. What was their name—Oglander, that was it. We must hunt up these Oglanders, and we ought also to make inquiries at Miss Drake's flat in Clarges Street.'

The following morning they paid their bill and departed somewhat crestfallen.

Hunting out the Oglanders was fairly easy with the aid of the telephone book. Tuppence this time took the offensive and assumed the character of a representative of a new illustrated paper. She called on Mrs Oglander, asking for a few details of their 'smart' supper party at the Savoy on Tuesday evening. These details Mrs Oglander was only too willing to supply. Just as she was leaving Tuppence added carelessly. 'Let me see, wasn't Miss Drake sitting at the table next to you? Is it really true that she is engaged to the Duke of Perth? You know her, of course.'

'I know her slightly,' said Mrs Oglander. 'A very charming girl, I believe. Yes, she was sitting at the next table to ours with Mr le Marchant. My girls know her better than I do.'

Tuppence's next port of call was the flat in Clarges

Street. Here she was greeted by Miss Marjory Leicester, the friend with whom Miss Drake shared a flat.

'Do tell me what all this is about?' asked Miss Leicester plaintively. 'Una has some deep game on and I don't know what it is. Of course she slept here on Tuesday night.'

'Did you see her when she came in?'

'No, I had gone to bed. She has got her own latch key, of course. She came in about one o'clock, I believe.'

'When did you see her?'

'Oh, the next morning about nine—or perhaps it was nearer ten.'

As Tuppence left the flat she almost collided with a tall gaunt female who was entering.

'Excuse me, Miss, I'm sure,' said the gaunt female.

'Do you work here?' asked Tuppence.

'Yes, Miss, I come daily.'

'What time do you get here in the morning?'

'Nine o'clock is my time, Miss.'

Tuppence slipped a hurried half-crown into the gaunt female's hand.

'Was Miss Drake here last Tuesday morning when you arrived?'

'Why, yes, Miss, indeed she was. Fast asleep in her bed and hardly woke up when I brought her in her tea.'

'Oh, thank you,' said Tuppence and went disconsolately down the stairs.

She had arranged to meet Tommy for lunch in a small restaurant in Soho and there they compared notes.

'I have seen that fellow Rice. It is quite true he did see Una Drake in the distance at Torquay.'

'Well,' said Tuppence, 'we have checked these alibis

all right. Here, give me a bit of paper and a pencil, Tommy. Let us put it down neatly like all detectives do.'

| 1.30 | Una Drake seen in Luncheon Car of train. |
| 4 o'clock | Arrives at Castle Hotel. |
| 5 o'clock | Seen by Mr Rice. |
| 8 o'clock | Seen dining at hotel. |
| 9.30 | Asks for hot water bottle. |
| 11.30 | Seen at Savoy with Mr le Marchant. |
| 7.30 a.m. | Called by chambermaid at Castle Hotel. |
| 9 o'clock. | Called by charwoman at flat at Clarges Street. |

They looked at each other.

'Well, it looks to me as if Blunt's Brilliant Detectives are beat,' said Tommy.

'Oh, we mustn't give up,' said Tuppence. 'Somebody *must* be lying!'

'The queer thing is that it strikes me nobody was lying. They all seemed perfectly truthful and straightforward.'

'Yet there must be a flaw. We know there is. I think of all sorts of things like private aeroplanes, but that doesn't really get us any forwarder.'

'I am inclined to the theory of an astral body.'

'Well,' said Tuppence, 'the only thing to do is to sleep on it. Your sub-conscious works in your sleep.'

'H'm,' said Tommy. 'If your sub-conscious provides you with a perfectly good answer to this riddle by tomorrow morning, I take off my hat to it.'

They were very silent all that evening. Again and again Tuppence reverted to the paper of times. She wrote things on bits of paper. She murmured to herself, she sought perplexedly through Rail Guides. But in the end they both rose to go to bed with no faint glimmer of light on the problem.

'This is very disheartening,' said Tommy.

'One of the most miserable evenings I have ever spent,' said Tuppence.

'We ought to have gone to a Music Hall,' said Tommy. 'A few good jokes about mothers-in-law and twins and bottles of beer would have done us no end of good.'

'No, you will see this concentration will work in the end,' said Tuppence. 'How busy our sub-conscious will have to be in the next eight hours!' And on this hopeful note they went to bed.

'Well,' said Tommy next morning. 'Has the subconscious worked?'

'I have got an idea,' said Tuppence.

'You have. What sort of an idea?'

'Well, rather a funny idea. Not at all like anything I have ever read in detective stories. As a matter of fact it is an idea that *you* put into my head.'

'Then it must be a good idea,' said Tommy firmly. 'Come on, Tuppence, out with it.'

'I shall have to send a cable to verify it,' said Tuppence. 'No, I am not going to tell you. It's a perfectly wild idea, but it's the only thing that fits the facts.'

'Well,' said Tommy, 'I must away to the office. A roomful of disappointed clients must not wait in vain. I leave this case in the hands of my promising subordinate.'

Tuppence nodded cheerfully.

She did not put in an appearance at the office all day.

When Tommy returned that evening about half-past five it was to find a wildly exultant Tuppence awaiting him.

'I have done it, Tommy. I have solved the mystery of the alibi. We can charge up all these half-crowns and ten-shilling notes and demand a substantial fee of our own from Mr Montgomery Jones and he can go right off and collect his girl.'

'What is the solution?' cried Tommy.

'A perfectly simple one,' said Tuppence. '*Twins*.'

'What do you mean?—Twins?'

'Why, just that. Of course it is the only solution. I will say you put it into my head last night talking about mothers-in-law, twins, and bottles of beer. I cabled to Australia and got back the information I wanted. Una has a twin sister, Vera, who arrived in England last Monday. That is why she was able to make this bet so spontaneously. She thought it would be a frightful rag on poor Montgomery Jones. The sister went to Torquay and she stayed in London.'

'Do you think she'll be terribly despondent that she's lost?' asked Tommy.

'No,' said Tuppence, 'I don't. I gave you my views about that before. She will put all the kudos down to Montgomery Jones. I always think respect for your husband's abilities should be the foundation of married life.'

'I am glad to have inspired these sentiments in you, Tuppence.'

'It is not a really satisfactory solution,' said Tuppence. 'Not the ingenious sort of flaw that Inspector French would have detected.'

'Nonsense,' said Tommy. 'I think the way I showed

these photographs to the waiter in the restaurant was exactly like Inspector French.'

'He didn't have to use nearly so many half-crowns and ten-shilling notes as we seem to have done,' said Tuppence.

'Never mind,' said Tommy. 'We can charge them all up with additions to Mr Montgomery Jones. He will be in such a state of idiotic bliss that he would probably pay the most enormous bill without jibbing at it.'

'So he should,' said Tuppence. 'Haven't Blunt's Brilliant Detectives been brilliantly successful? Oh, Tommy, I do think we are extraordinarily clever. It quite frightens me sometimes.'

'The next case we have shall be a Roger Sheringham case, and you, Tuppence, shall be Roger Sheringham.'

'I shall have to talk a lot,' said Tuppence.

'You do that naturally,' said Tommy. 'And now I suggest that we carry out my programme of last night and seek out a Music Hall where they have plenty of jokes about mothers-in-law, bottles of beer, *and Twins*.'

# The Case of the Missing Will

The problem presented to us by Miss Violet Marsh made rather a pleasant change from our usual routine work. Poirot had received a brisk and business-like note from the lady asking for an appointment, and he had replied asking her to call upon him at eleven o'clock the following day.

She arrived punctually—a tall, handsome young woman, plainly but neatly dressed, with an assured and business-like manner. Clearly a young woman who meant to get on in the world. I am not a great admirer of the so-called New Woman myself, and, in spite of her good looks, I was not particularly prepossessed in her favour.

'My business is of a somewhat unusual nature, Monsieur Poirot,' she began, after she had accepted a chair. 'I had better begin at the beginning and tell you the whole story.'

'If you please, mademoiselle.'

'I am an orphan. My father was one of two brothers, sons of a small yeoman farmer in Devonshire. The farm was a poor one, and the elder brother, Andrew, emigrated to Australia, where he did very well indeed, and by means of successful speculation in land became a very rich man. The younger brother, Roger (my father), had no leanings towards the agricultural life. He managed to educate himself a little, and obtained a post as clerk with a small firm. He married slightly above him; my mother was the daughter of a poor artist. My father died when I was six years old. When I was fourteen, my mother followed him to the grave. My only living relation then was my Uncle Andrew, who had recently returned from Australia and bought a small place, Crabtree Manor, in his native county. He was exceedingly kind to his brother's orphan child, took me to live with him, and treated me in every way as though I was his own daughter.

'Crabtree Manor, in spite of its name, is really only an old farmhouse. Farming was in my uncle's blood, and he was intensely interested in various modern farming experiments. Although kindness itself to me, he had certain peculiar and deeply-rooted ideas as to the upbringing of women. Himself a man of little or no education, though possessing remarkable shrewdness, he placed little value on what he called "book knowledge". He was especially opposed to the education of women. In his opinion, girls should learn practical housework and dairy-work, be useful about the home, and have as little to do with book learning as possible. He proposed to bring me up on these lines, to my bitter disappointment and annoyance. I rebelled frankly. I knew that I possessed a good brain, and had absolutely no talent for domestic duties. My uncle and I had many bitter arguments on the subject, for, though much attached to each other, we were both self-willed. I was lucky enough to win a scholarship, and up to a certain point was successful in getting my own way. The crisis arose when I resolved to go to Girton. I had a little money of my own, left me by my mother, and I was quite determined to make the best use of the gifts God had given me. I had one long, final argument with my uncle. He put the facts plainly before me. He had no other relations, and he had intended me to be his sole heiress. As I have told you, he was a very rich man. If I persisted in these "new-fangled notions" of mine, however, I need look for nothing from him. I remained polite, but firm. I should always be deeply attached to him, I told him, but I must lead my own life. We parted on that note. "You fancy your brains, my girl," were his last words. "I've no book learning, but, for all that, I'll pit mine against yours any day. We'll see what we shall see."'

'That was nine years ago. I have stayed with him for a weekend occasionally, and our relations were perfectly amicable, though his views remained unaltered. He never referred to my having matriculated, nor to my BSc. For the last three years his health had been failing, and a month ago he died.

'I am now coming to the point of my visit. My uncle left a most extraordinary will. By its terms, Crabtree Manor and its contents are to be at my disposal for a year from his death—"during which time my clever niece may prove her wits", the actual words run. At the end of that period, "my wits having been proved better than hers", the house and all my uncle's large fortune pass to various charitable institutions.'

'That is a little hard on you, mademoiselle, seeing that you were Mr Marsh's only blood relation.'

'I do not look on it in that way. Uncle Andrew warned me fairly, and I chose my own path. Since I would not fall in with his wishes, he was at perfect liberty to leave his money to whom he pleased.'

'Was the will drawn up by a lawyer?'

'No; it was written on a printed will-form and witnessed by the man and his wife who live at the house and do for my uncle.'

'There might be a possibility of upsetting such a will?'

'I would not even attempt to do such a thing.'

'You regard it then as a sporting challenge on the part of your uncle?'

'That is exactly how I look upon it.'

'It bears that interpretation, certainly,' said Poirot thoughtfully. 'Somewhere in this rambling old manor-house your uncle has concealed either a sum of money in notes or possibly a second will, and has given you a year in which to exercise your ingenuity to find it.'

'Exactly, Monsieur Poirot; and I am paying you the compliment of assuming that your ingenuity will be greater than mine.'

'Eh, eh! but that is very charming of you. My grey cells are at your disposal. You have made no search yourself?'

'Only a cursory one; but I have too much respect for my uncle's undoubted abilities to fancy that the task will be an easy one.'

'Have you the will or a copy of it with you?'

Miss March handed a document across the table. Poirot ran through it, nodding to himself.

'Made three years ago. Dated March 25; and the time is given also—11 a.m.—that is very suggestive. It narrows the field of search. Assuredly it is another will we have to seek for. A will made even half an hour later would upset this. *Eh bien*, mademoiselle, it is a problem charming and ingenious that you have presented to me here. I shall have all the pleasure in the world in solving it for you. Granted that your uncle was a man of ability, his grey cells cannot have been of the quality of Hercule Poirot's!'

(Really, Poirot's vanity is blatant!)

'Fortunately, I have nothing of moment on hand at the minute. Hastings and I will go down to Crabtree Manor tonight. The man and wife who attended on your uncle are still there, I presume?'

'Yes, their name is Baker.'

The following morning saw us started on the hunt proper. We had arrived late the night before. Mr and Mrs Baker, having received a telegram from Miss Marsh, were expecting us. They were a pleasant couple, the man gnarled and pink-cheeked, like a shrivelled pippin, and his wife a woman of vast proportion and true Devonshire calm.

Tired with our journey and the eight-mile drive from the station, we had retired at once to bed after a supper of roast chicken, apple pie, and Devonshire cream. We had now disposed of an excellent breakfast, and were sitting in a small panelled room which had been the late Mr Marsh's study and living room. A roll-top desk stuffed with papers, all neatly docketed, stood against the wall, and a big leather armchair showed plainly that it had been its owner's constant resting-place. A big chintz-covered settee ran along the opposite wall, and the deep low window seats were covered with the same faded chintz of an old-fashioned pattern.

'*Eh bien, mon ami,*' said Poirot, lighting one of his tiny cigarettes, 'we must map out our plan of campaign. Already I have made a rough survey of the house, but I am of the opinion that any clue will be found in this room. We shall have to go through the documents in the desk with meticulous care. Naturally, I do not expect to find the will amongst them, but it is likely that some apparently innocent paper may conceal the clue to its hiding-place. But first we must have a little information. Ring the bell, I pray of you.'

I did so. While we were waiting for it to be answered, Poirot walked up and down, looking about him approvingly.

'A man of method, this Mr Marsh. See how neatly the packets of papers are docketed; then the key to each drawer has its ivory label—so has the key of the china cabinet on the wall; and see with what precision the china within is arranged. It rejoices the heart. Nothing here offends the eye—'

He came to an abrupt pause, as his eye was caught by the key of the desk itself, to which a dirty envelope was affixed. Poirot frowned at it and withdrew it from the lock. On it were scrawled the words: 'Key of Roll Top Desk,' in a crabbed handwriting, quite unlike the neat superscriptions on the other keys.

'An alien note,' said Poirot, frowning. 'I could swear that here we have no longer the personality of Mr Marsh. But who else has been in the house? Only Miss Marsh, and she, if I mistake not, is also a young lady of method and order.'

Baker came in answer to the bell.

'Will you fetch madame your wife, and answer a few questions?'

Baker departed, and in a few moments returned with Mrs Baker, wiping her hands on her apron and beaming all over her face.

In a few clear words Poirot set forth the object of his mission. The Bakers were immediately sympathetic.

'Us don't want to see Miss Violet done out of what's hers,' declared the woman. 'Cruel hard 'twould be for hospitals to get it all.'

Poirot proceeded with his questions. Yes, Mr and Mrs Baker remembered perfectly witnessing the will. Baker had previously been sent into the neighbouring town to get two printed will-forms.

'Two?' said Poirot sharply.

'Yes, sir, for safety like, I suppose, in case he should spoil one—and sure enough, so he did do. Us had signed one—'

'What time of day was that?'

Baker scratched his head, but his wife was quicker.

'Why, to be sure, I'd just put the milk on for the cocoa at eleven. Don't ee remember? It had all boiled over on the stove when us got back to kitchen.'

'And afterwards?'

''Twould be about an hour later. Us had to go in again. "I've made a mistake," says old master, "had to tear the whole thing up. I'll trouble you to sign again," and us did. And afterwards master gave us a tidy sum of money each. "I've left you nothing in my will," says he, "but each year I live you'll have this to be a nest-egg when I'm gone"—and sure enough, so he did.'

Poirot reflected.

'After you had signed the second time, what did Mr Marsh do? Do you know?'

'Went out to the village to pay tradesmen's books.'

That did not seem very promising. Poirot tried another tack. He held out the key of the desk.

'Is that your master's writing?'

I may have imagined it, but I fancied that a moment or two elapsed before Baker replied: 'Yes, sir, it is.'

'He's lying,' I thought. 'But why?'

'Has your master let the house?—have there been any strangers in it during the last three years?'

'No, sir.'

'No visitors?' 'Only Miss Violet.'

'No strangers of any kind been inside this room?'

'No, sir.'

'You forget the workmen, Jim,' his wife reminded him.

'Workmen?' Poirot wheeled round on her. 'What workmen?'

The woman explained that about two years and a half ago workmen had been in the house to do certain repairs. She was quite vague as to what the repairs were. Her view seemed to be that the whole thing was a fad of her master's and quite unnecessary. Part of the time the workmen had been in the study; but what they had done there she could not say, as her master had not let either of them into the room whilst the work was in progress. Unfortunately, they could not remember the name of the firm employed, beyond the fact that it was a Plymouth one.

'We progress, Hastings,' said Poirot, rubbing his hands as the Bakers left the room. 'Clearly he made a second will and then had workmen from Plymouth in to make a suitable hiding-place. Instead of wasting time taking up the floor and tapping the walls, we will go to Plymouth.'

With a little trouble, we were able to get the information we wanted. After one or two essays we found the firm employed by Mr Marsh.

Their employees had all been with them many years, and it was easy to find the two men who had worked under Mr Marsh's orders. They remembered the job perfectly. Amongst various other minor jobs, they had taken up one of the bricks of the old-fashioned fireplace, made a cavity beneath, and so cut the brick that it was impossible to see the join. By pressing on the second brick from the end, the whole thing was raised. It had been quite a complicated piece of work, and the old gentleman had been very fussy about it. Our informant was a man called Coghan, a big, gaunt man with a grizzled moustache. He seemed an intelligent fellow.

We returned to Crabtree Manor in high spirits, and, locking the study door, proceeded to put our newly acquired knowledge into effect. It was impossible to see any sign on the bricks, but when we pressed in the manner indicated, a deep cavity was at once disclosed.

Eagerly Poirot plunged in his hand. Suddenly his face fell from complacent elation to consternation. All he held was a charred fragment of stiff paper. But for it, the cavity was empty.

'*Sacre!*' cried Poirot angrily. 'Someone has been before us.'

We examined the scrap of paper anxiously. Clearly it was a fragment of what we sought. A portion of Baker's signature remained, but no indication of what the terms of the will had been.

Poirot sat back on his heels. His expression would have been comical if we had not been so overcome. 'I understand it not,' he growled. 'Who destroyed this? And what was their object?'

'The Bakers?' I suggested.

'*Pourquoi?* Neither will makes any provision for them, and they are more likely to be kept on with Miss Marsh than if the place became the property of a hospital. How could it be to anyone's advantage to destroy the will? The hospitals benefit—yes; but one cannot suspect institutions.'

'Perhaps the old man changed his mind and destroyed it himself,' I suggested.

Poirot rose to his feet, dusting his knees with his usual care.

'That may be,' he admitted, 'one of your more sensible observations, Hastings. Well, we can do no more here. We have done all that mortal man can do. We have successfully pitted our wits against the late Andrew Marsh's; but, unfortunately, his niece is not better off for our success.'

By driving to the station at once, we were just able to catch a train to London, though not the principal express. Poirot was sad and dissatisfied. For my part, I was tired and dozed in a corner. Suddenly, as we were just moving out of Taunton, Poirot uttered a piercing squeal.

'*Vite*, Hastings! Awake and jump! But jump I say!'

Before I knew where I was we were standing on the platform, bareheaded and minus our valises, whilst the train disappeared into the night. I was furious. But Poirot paid no attention.

'Imbecile that I have been!' he cried. 'Triple imbecile! Not again will I vaunt my little grey cells!'

'That's a good job at any rate,' I said grumpily. 'But what is this all about?'

As usual, when following out his own ideas, Poirot paid absolutely no attention to me.

'The tradesmen's books—I have left them entirely out of account! Yes, but where? Where? Never mind, I cannot be mistaken. We must return at once.'

Easier said than done. We managed to get a slow train to Exeter, and there Poirot hired a car. We arrived back at Crabtree Manor in the small hours of the morning. I pass over the bewilderment of the Bakers when we had at last aroused them. Paying no attention to anybody, Poirot strode at once to the study.

'I have been, not a triple imbecile, but thirty-six times one, my friend,' he deigned to remark. 'Now, behold!'

Going straight to the desk he drew out the key, and detached the envelope from it. I stared at him stupidly. How could he possibly hope to find a big will-form in that tiny envelope? With great care he cut open the envelope, laying it out flat. Then he lighted the fire and held the plain inside surface of the envelope to the flame. In a few minutes faint characters began to appear.

'Look, *mon ami!*' cried Poirot in triumph.

I looked. There were just a few lines of faint writing stating briefly that he left everything to his niece, Violet Marsh. It was dated March 25, 12.30 p.m., and witnessed by Albert Pike, confectioner, and Jessie Pike, married woman.

'But is it legal?' I gasped.

'As far as I know, there is no law against writing your will in a blend of disappearing and sympathetic ink. The intention of the testator is clear, and the beneficiary is his only living relation. But the cleverness of him! He foresaw every step that a searcher would take—that I, miserable imbecile, took. He gets two will-forms, makes the servants sign twice, then sallies out with his will written on the inside of a dirty envelope and a fountain-pen containing his little ink mixture. On some excuse he gets the confectioner and his wife to sign their names under his own signature, then he ties it to the key of his desk and chuckles to himself. If his niece sees through his little ruse, she will have justified her choice of life and elaborate education and be thoroughly welcome to his money.'

'She didn't see through it, did she?' I said slowly. 'It seems rather unfair. The old man really won.'

'But no, Hastings. It is *your* wits that go astray. Miss Marsh proved the astuteness of her wits and the value of the higher education for women by at once putting the matter in *my* hands. Always employ the expert. She has amply proved her right to the money.'

I wonder—I very much wonder—what old Andrew Marsh would have thought!

# Ingots of Gold

'I do not know that the story that I am going to tell you is a fair one,' said Raymond West, 'because I can't give you the solution of it. Yet the facts were so interesting and so curious that I should like to propound it to you as a problem. And perhaps between us we may arrive at some logical conclusion.

'The date of these happenings was two years ago, when I went down to spend Whitsuntide with a man called John Newman, in Cornwall.'

'Cornwall?' said Joyce Lemprière sharply.

'Yes. Why?'

'Nothing. Only it's odd. My story is about a place in Cornwall, too—a little fishing village called Rathole. Don't tell me yours is the same?'

'No. My village is called Polperran. It is situated on the west coast of Cornwall; a very wild and rocky spot. I had been introduced a few weeks previously and had found him a most interesting companion. A man of intelligence and independent means, he was possessed of a romantic imagination. As a result of his latest hobby he had taken the lease of Pol House. He was an authority on Elizabethan times, and he described to me in vivid and graphic language the rout of the Spanish Armada. So enthusiastic was he that one could almost imagine that he had been an eyewitness at the scene. Is there anything in reincarnation? I wonder—I very much wonder.'

'You are so romantic, Raymond dear,' said Miss Marple, looking benignantly at him.

'Romantic is the last thing that I am,' said Raymond West, slightly annoyed. 'But this fellow Newman was chock-full of it, and he interested me for that reason as a curious survival of the past. It appears that a certain ship belonging to the Armada, and known to contain a vast amount of treasure in the form of gold from the Spanish Main, was wrecked off the coast of Cornwall on the famous and treacherous Serpent Rocks. For some years, so Newman told me, attempts had been made to salve the ship and recover the treasure. I believe such stories are not uncommon, though the number of mythical treasure ships is largely in excess of the genuine ones. A company had been formed, but had gone bankrupt, and Newman had been able to buy the rights of the thing— or whatever you call it—for a mere song. He waxed very enthusiastic about it all. According to him it was merely a question of the latest scientific, up-to-date machinery. The gold was there, and he had no doubt whatever that it could be recovered.

'It occurred to me as I listened to him how often things happen that way. A rich man such as Newman succeeds almost without effort, and yet in all probability the actual value in money of his find would mean little to him. I must say that his ardour infected me. I saw galleons drifting up the coast, flying before the storm, beaten and broken on the black rocks. The mere word galleon has a romantic sound. The phrase "Spanish Gold" thrills the schoolboy—and the grown-up man also. Moreover, I was working at the time upon a novel, some scenes of which were laid in the sixteenth century, and I saw the prospect of getting valuable local colour from my host.

'I set off that Friday morning from Paddington in high spirits, and looking forward to my trip. The carriage was empty except for one man, who sat facing me in the opposite corner. He was a tall, soldierly-looking man, and I could not rid myself of the impression that somewhere or other I had seen him before. I cudgelled my brains for some time in vain; but at last I had it. My travelling companion was Inspector Badgworth, and I had run across him when I was doing a series of articles on the Everson disappearance case.

'I recalled myself to his notice, and we were soon chatting pleasantly enough. When I told him I was going to Polperran he remarked that that was a rum coincidence, because he himself was also bound for that place. I did not like to seem inquisitive, so was careful not to ask him what took him there. Instead, I spoke of my own interest in the place, and mentioned the wrecked Spanish galleon. To my surprise the Inspector seemed to know all about it. "That will be the *Juan Fernandez*," he said. "Your friend won't be the first who has sunk money trying to get money out of her. It is a romantic notion."

'"And probably the whole story is a myth," I said. "No ship was ever wrecked there at all."

"'Oh, the ship was sunk there right enough," said the Inspector—"along with a good company of others. You would be surprised if you knew how many wrecks there are on that part of the coast. As a matter of fact, that is what takes me down there now. That is where the *Otranto* was wrecked six months ago."

"'I remember reading about it," I said. "No lives were lost, I think?"

"'No lives were lost," said the Inspector; "but something else was lost. It is not generally known, but the *Otranto* was carrying bullion."

"'Yes?" I said, much interested.

"'Naturally we have had divers at work on salvage operations, but—*the gold has gone, Mr West.*"

"'Gone!" I said, staring at him. "How can it have gone?"

"'That is the question," said the Inspector. "The rocks tore a gaping hole in her strongroom. It was easy enough for the divers to get in that way, but they found the strong-room empty. The question is, was the gold stolen before the wreck or afterwards? Was it ever in the strongroom at all?"

"'It seems a curious case," I said.

"'It is a very curious case, when you consider what bullion is. Not a diamond necklace that you could put into your pocket. When you think how cumbersome it is and how bulky—well, the whole thing seems absolutely impossible. There may have been some hocus-pocus before the ship sailed; but if not, it must have been removed within the last six months—and I am going down to look into the matter."

'I found Newman waiting to meet me at the station.

He apologized for the absence of his car, which had gone to Truro for some necessary repairs. Instead, he met me with a farm lorry belonging to the property.

'I swung myself up beside him, and we wound carefully in and out of the narrow streets of the fishing village. We went up a steep ascent, with a gradient, I should say, of one in five, ran a little distance along a winding lane, and turned in at the granite-pillared gates of Pol House.

'The place was a charming one; it was situated high up the cliffs, with a good view out to sea. Part of it was some three or four hundred years old, and a modern wing had been added. Behind it farming land of about seven or eight acres ran inland.

'"Welcome to Pol House," said Newman. "And to the Sign of the Golden Galleon." And he pointed to where, over the front door, hung a perfect reproduction of a Spanish galleon with all sails set.

'My first evening was a most charming and instructive one. My host showed me the old manuscripts relating to the *Juan Fernandez*. He unrolled charts for me and indicated positions on them with dotted lines, and he produced plans of diving apparatus, which, I may say, mystified me utterly and completely.

'I told him of my meeting with Inspector Badgworth, in which he was much interested.

'"They are a queer people round this coast," he said reflectively. "Smuggling and wrecking is in their blood. When a ship goes down on their coast they cannot help regarding it as lawful plunder meant for their pockets. There is a fellow here I should like you to see. He is an interesting survival."

'Next day dawned bright and clear. I was taken down into Polperran and there introduced to Newman's diver, a man called Higgins. He was a wooden-faced individual, extremely taciturn, and his contributions to the conversation were mostly monosyllables. After a discussion between them on highly technical matters, we adjourned to the Three Anchors. A tankard of beer somewhat loosened the worthy fellow's tongue.

'"Detective gentleman from London has come down," he grunted. "They do say that that ship that went down there last November was carrying a mortal lot of gold. Well, she wasn't the first to go down, and she won't be the last."

'"Hear, hear," chimed in the landlord of the Three Anchors. "That is a true word you say there, Bill Higgins."

'"I reckon it is, Mr Kelvin," said Higgins.

'I looked with some curiosity at the landlord. He was a remarkable-looking man, dark and swarthy, with curiously broad shoulders. His eyes were bloodshot, and he had a curiously furtive way of avoiding one's glance. I suspected that this was the man of whom Newman had spoken, saying he was an interesting survival.

'"We don't want interfering foreigners on this coast," he said, somewhat truculently.

'"Meaning the police?" asked Newman, smiling.

'"Meaning the police—*and others*," said Kelvin significantly. "And don't you forget it, mister."

'"Do you know, Newman, that sounded to me very like a threat," I said as we climbed the hill homewards.

'My friend laughed.

'"Nonsense; I don't do the folk down here any harm."

59

'I shook my head doubtfully. There was something sinister and uncivilized about Kelvin. I felt that his mind might run in strange, unrecognized channels.

'I think I date the beginning of my uneasiness from that moment. I had slept well enough that first night, but the next night my sleep was troubled and broken. Sunday dawned, dark and sullen, with an overcast sky and the threatenings of thunder in the air. I am always a bad hand at hiding my feelings, and Newman noticed the change in me.

'"What is the matter with you, West? You are a bundle of nerves this morning."

'"I don't know," I confessed, "but I have got a horrible feeling of foreboding."

'"It's the weather."

'"Yes, perhaps."

'I said no more. In the afternoon we went out in Newman's motor boat, but the rain came on with such vigour that we were glad to return to shore and change into dry clothing.

'And that evening my uneasiness increased. Outside the storm howled and roared. Towards ten o'clock the tempest calmed down. Newman looked out of the window.

'"It is clearing," he said. "I shouldn't wonder if it was a perfectly fine night in another half-hour. If so, I shall go out for a stroll."

'I yawned. "I am frightfully sleepy," I said. "I didn't get much sleep last night. I think that tonight I shall turn in early."

'This I did. On the previous night I had slept little. Tonight I slept heavily. Yet my slumbers were not restful. I was still oppressed with an awful foreboding of evil; I had terrible dreams. I dreamt of dreadful abysses and vast chasms, amongst which I was wandering, knowing that a slip of the foot meant death. I waked to find the hands of my clock pointing to eight o'clock. My head was aching badly, and the terror of my night's dreams was still upon me.

'So strongly was this so that when I went to the window and drew it up I started back with a fresh feeling of terror, for the first thing I saw, or thought I saw—was a man digging an open grave.

'It took me a minute or two to pull myself together; then I realized that the grave-digger was Newman's gardener, and the "grave" was destined to accommodate three new rose trees which were lying on the turf waiting for the moment they should be securely planted in the earth.

'The gardener looked up and saw me and touched his hat.

'"Good morning, sir. Nice morning, sir."

'"I suppose it is," I said doubtfully, still unable to shake off completely the depression of my spirits.

'However, as the gardener had said, it was certainly a nice morning. The sun was shining and the sky a clear pale blue that promised fine weather for the day. I went down to breakfast whistling a tune. Newman had no maids living in the house. Two middle-aged sisters, who lived in a farm-house near by, came daily to attend to his simple wants. One of them was placing the coffee-pot on the table as I entered the room.

'"Good morning, Elizabeth," I said. "Mr Newman not down yet?"

'"He must have been out very early, sir," she replied. "He wasn't in the house when we arrived."

'Instantly my uneasiness returned. On the two previous mornings Newman had come down to breakfast somewhat late; and I didn't fancy that at any time he was an early riser. Moved by those forebodings, I ran up to his bedroom. It was empty, and, moreover, his bed had not been slept in. A brief examination of his room showed me two other things. If Newman had gone out for a stroll he must have gone out in his evening clothes, for they were missing.

'I was sure now that my premonition of evil was justified. Newman had gone, as he had said he would do— for an evening stroll. For some reason or other he had not returned. Why? Had he met with an accident? Fallen over the cliffs? A search must be made at once.

'In a few hours I had collected a large band of helpers, and together we hunted in every direction along the cliffs and on the rocks below. But there was no sign of Newman.

'In the end, in despair, I sought out Inspector Badgworth. His face grew very grave.

'"It looks to me as if there has been foul play," he said. "There are some not over-scrupulous customers in these parts. Have you seen Kelvin, the landlord of the Three Anchors?"

'I said that I had seen him.

'"Did you know he did a turn in gaol four years ago? Assault and battery."

'"It doesn't surprise me," I said.

'"The general opinion in this place seems to be that your friend is a bit too fond of nosing his way into things that do not concern him. I hope he has come to no serious harm."

'The search was continued with redoubled vigour. It was not until late that afternoon that our efforts were rewarded. We discovered Newman in a deep ditch in a corner of his own property. His hands and feet were securely fastened with rope, and a handkerchief had been thrust into his mouth and secured there so as to prevent him crying out.

'He was terribly exhausted and in great pain; but after some frictioning of his wrists and ankles, and a long draught from a whisky flask, he was able to give his account of what had occurred.

'The weather having cleared, he had gone out for a stroll about eleven o'clock. His way had taken him some distance along the cliffs to a spot commonly known as Smugglers' Cove, owing to the large number of caves to be found there. Here he had noticed some men landing something from a small boat, and had strolled down to see what was going on. Whatever the stuff was it seemed to be a great weight, and it was being carried into one of the farthermost caves.

'With no real suspicion of anything being amiss, nevertheless Newman had wondered. He had drawn quite near them without being observed. Suddenly there was a cry of alarm, and immediately two powerful seafaring men had set upon him and rendered him unconscious. When next he came to himself he found himself lying on a motor vehicle of some kind, which was proceeding, with many bumps and bangs, as far as he could guess, up the lane which led from the coast to the village. To his great surprise, the lorry turned in at the gate of his own house. There, after a whispered conversation between the men, they at length drew him forth and flung him into a ditch at a spot where the depth of it rendered discovery unlikely for some time. Then the lorry drove on, and, he thought, passed out through another gate some quarter of a mile nearer the village. He could give no description of his assailants except that they were certainly seafaring men and, by their speech, Cornishmen.

'Inspector Badgworth was very interested.

'"Depend upon it that is where the stuff has been hidden," he cried. "Somehow or other it has been salvaged from the wreck and has been stored in some lonely cave somewhere. It is known that we have searched all the caves in Smugglers' Cove, and that we are now going farther afield, and they have evidently been moving the stuff at night to a cave that has been already searched and is not likely to be searched again. Unfortunately they have had at least eighteen hours to dispose of the stuff. If they got Mr Newman last night I doubt if we will find any of it there by now."

'The Inspector hurried off to make a search. He found definite evidence that the bullion had been stored as supposed, but the gold had been once more removed, and there was no clue as to its fresh hiding-place.

'One clue there was, however, and the Inspector himself pointed it out to me the following morning.

'"That lane is very little used by motor vehicles," he said, "and in one or two places we get the traces of the tyres very clearly. There is a three-cornered piece out of one tyre, leaving a mark which is quite unmistakable. It shows going into the gate; here and there is a faint mark of it going out of the other gate, so there is not much doubt that it is the right vehicle we are after. Now, why did they take it out through the farther gate? It seems quite clear to me that the lorry came from the village. Now, there aren't many people who own a lorry in the village—not more than two or three at most. Kelvin, the landlord of the Three Anchors, has one."

"'What was Kelvin's original profession?" asked Newman.

"'It is curious that you should ask me that, Mr Newman. In his young days Kelvin was a professional diver."

'Newman and I looked at each other. The puzzle seemed to be fitting itself together piece by piece.

"'You didn't recognize Kelvin as one of the men on the beach?" asked the Inspector.

'Newman shook his head.

"'I am afraid I can't say anything as to that," he said regretfully. "I really hadn't time to see anything."

'The Inspector very kindly allowed me to accompany him to the Three Anchors. The garage was up a side street. The big doors were closed, but by going up a little alley at the side we found a small door that led into it, and the door was open. A very brief examination of the tyres sufficed for the Inspector. "We have got him, by Jove!" he exclaimed. "Here is the mark as large as life on the rear left wheel. Now, Mr Kelvin, I don't think you will be clever enough to wriggle out of this."'

Raymond West came to a halt.

'Well?' said Joyce. 'So far I don't see anything to make a problem about—unless they never found the gold.'

'They never found the gold certainly,' said Raymond,

'and they never got Kelvin either. I expect he was too clever for them, but I don't quite see how he worked it. He was duly arrested—on the evidence of the tyre mark. But an extraordinary hitch arose. Just opposite the big doors of the garage was a cottage rented for the summer by a lady artist.'

'Oh, these lady artists!' said Joyce, laughing.

'As you say, "Oh, these lady artists!" This particular one had been ill for some weeks, and, in consequence, had two hospital nurses attending her. The nurse who was on night duty had pulled her armchair up to the window, where the blind was up. She declared that the motor lorry could not have left the garage opposite without her seeing it, and she swore that in actual fact it never left the garage that night.'

'I don't think that is much of a problem,' said Joyce. 'The nurse went to sleep, of course. They always do.'

'That has—er—been known to happen,' said Mr Petherick, judiciously; 'but it seems to me that we are accepting facts without sufficient examination. Before accepting the testimony of the hospital nurse, we should inquire very closely into her bona fides. The alibi coming with such suspicious promptness is inclined to raise doubts in one's mind.'

'There is also the lady artist's testimony,' said Raymond. 'She declared that she was in pain, and awake most of the night, and that she would certainly have heard the lorry, it being an unusual noise, and the night being very quiet after the storm.'

'H'm,' said the clergyman, 'that is certainly an additional fact. Had Kelvin himself any alibi?'

'He declared that he was at home and in bed from ten

o'clock onwards, but he could produce no witnesses in support of that statement.'

'The nurse went to sleep,' said Joyce, 'and so did the patient. Ill people always think they have never slept a wink all night.'

Raymond West looked inquiringly at Dr Pender.

'Do you know, I feel very sorry for that man Kelvin. It seems to me very much a case of "Give a dog a bad name." Kelvin had been in prison. Apart from the tyre mark, which certainly seems too remarkable to be coincidence, there doesn't seem to be much against him except his unfortunate record.'

'You, Sir Henry?'

Sir Henry shook his head.

'As it happens,' he said, smiling, 'I know something about this case. So clearly I mustn't speak.'

'Well, go on, Aunt Jane; haven't you got anything to say?'

'In a minute, dear,' said Miss Marple. 'I am afraid I have counted wrong. Two purl, three plain, slip one, two purl—yes, that's right. What did you say, dear?'

'What is your opinion?'

'You wouldn't like my opinion, dear. Young people never do, I notice. It is better to say nothing.'

'Nonsense, Aunt Jane; out with it.'

'Well, dear Raymond,' said Miss Marple, laying down her knitting and looking across at her nephew. 'I do think you should be more careful how you choose your friends. You are so credulous, dear, so easily gulled. I suppose it is being a writer and having so much imagination. All that story about a Spanish galleon! If you were older and had more experience of life you would have been on your guard at once. A man you had known only a few weeks, too!'

Sir Henry suddenly gave vent to a great roar of laughter and slapped his knee.

'Got you this time, Raymond,' he said. 'Miss Marple, you are wonderful. Your friend Newman, my boy, has another name—several other names in fact. At the present moment he is not in Cornwall but in Devonshire—Dartmoor, to be exact—a convict in Princetown prison. We didn't catch him over the stolen bullion business, but over the rifling of the strongroom of one of the London banks. Then we looked up his past record and we found a good portion of the gold stolen buried in the garden at Pol House. It was rather a neat idea. All along that Cornish coast there are stories of wrecked galleons full of gold. It accounted for the diver and it would account later for the gold. But a scapegoat was needed, and Kelvin was ideal for the purpose. Newman played his little comedy very well, and our friend Raymond, with his celebrity as a writer, made an unimpeachable witness.'

'But the tyre mark?' objected Joyce.

'Oh, I saw that at once, dear, although I know nothing about motors,' said Miss Marple. 'People change a wheel, you know—I have often seen them doing it—and, of course, they could take a wheel off Kelvin's lorry and take it out through the small door into the alley and put it on to Mr Newman's lorry and take the lorry out of one gate down to the beach, fill it up with the gold and bring it up through the other gate, and then they must have taken the wheel back and put it back on Mr Kelvin's lorry while, I suppose, someone else was tying up Mr Newman in a ditch. Very uncomfortable for him and probably longer before he was found than he expected. I suppose the man who called himself the gardener attended to that side of the business.'

'Why do you say, "called himself the gardener," Aunt Jane?' asked Raymond curiously.

'Well, he can't have been a real gardener, can he?' said Miss Marple. 'Gardeners don't work on Whit Monday. Everybody knows that.'

She smiled and folded up her knitting.

'It was really that little fact that put me on the right scent,' she said. She looked across at Raymond.

'When you are a householder, dear, and have a garden of your own, you will know these little things.'

# Double Sin

I had called in at my friend Poirot's rooms to find him sadly overworked. So much had he become the rage that every rich woman who had mislaid a bracelet or lost a pet kitten rushed to secure the services of the great Hercule Poirot. My little friend was a strange mixture of Flemish thrift and artistic fervour. He accepted many cases in which he had little interest owing to the first instinct being predominant.

He also undertook cases in which there was a little or no monetary reward sheerly because the problem involved interested him. The result was that, as I say, he was overworking himself. He admitted as much himself, and I found little difficulty in persuading him to accompany me for a week's holiday to that well-known South Coast resort, Ebermouth.

We had spent four very agreeable days when Poirot came to me, an open letter in his hand.

'*Mon ami*, you remember my friend Joseph Aarons, the theatrical agent?'

I assented after a moment's thought. Poirot's friends are so many and so varied, and range from dustmen to dukes.

'*Eh bien*, Hastings, Joseph Aarons finds himself at Charlock Bay. He is far from well, and there is a little affair that it seems is worrying him. He begs me to go over and see him. I think, *mon ami*, that I must accede to his request. He is a faithful friend, the good Joseph Aarons, and has done much to assist me in the past.'

'Certainly, if you think so,' I said. 'I believe Charlock Bay is a beautiful spot, and as it happens I've never been there.'

'Then we combine business with pleasure,' said Poirot. 'You will inquire the trains, yes?'

'It will probably mean a change or two,' I said with a grimace. 'You know what these cross-country lines are. To go from the South Devon Coast to the North Devon coast is sometimes a day's journey.'

However, on inquiry, I found that the journey could be accomplished by only one change at Exeter and that the trains were good. I was hastening back to Poirot with the information when I happened to pass the offices of the Speedy cars and saw written up:

*Tomorrow. All-day excursion to Charlock Bay. Starting 8.30 through some of the most beautiful scenery in Devon.*

I inquired a few particulars and returned to the hotel full of enthusiasm. Unfortunately, I found it hard to make Poirot share my feelings.

'My friend, why this passion for the motor coach? The train, see you, it is sure? The tyres, they do not burst; the accidents, they do not happen. One is not incommoded by too much air. The windows can be shut and no draughts admitted.'

71

I hinted delicately that the advantage of fresh air was what attracted me most to the motor-coach scheme.

'And if it rains? Your English climate is so uncertain.'

'There's a hood and all that. Besides, if it rains badly, the excursion doesn't take place.'

'Ah!' said Poirot. 'Then let us hope that it rains.'

'Of course, if you feel like that and…'

'No, no, *mon ami*. I see that you have set your heart on the trip. Fortunately, I have my greatcoat with me and two mufflers.' He sighed. 'But shall we have sufficient time at Charlock Bay?'

'Well, I'm afraid it means staying the night there. You see, the tour goes round by Dartmoor. We have lunch at Monkhampton. We arrive at Charlock Bay about four o'clock, and the coach starts back at five, arriving here at ten o'clock.'

'So!' said Poirot. 'And there are people who do this for pleasure! We shall, of course, get a reduction of the fare since we do not make the return journey?'

'I hardly think that's likely.'

'You must insist.'

'Come now, Poirot, don't be mean. You know you're coining money.'

'My friend, it is not the meanness. It is the business sense. If I were a millionaire, I would pay only what was just and right.'

As I had foreseen, however, Poirot was doomed to fail in this respect. The gentleman who issued tickets at the Speedy office was calm and unimpassioned but adamant. His point was that we ought to return. He even implied that we ought to pay extra for the privilege of leaving the coach at Charlock Bay.

Defeated, Poirot paid over the required sum and left the office.

'The English, they have no sense of money,' he grumbled. 'Did you observe a young man, Hastings, who paid over the full fare and yet mentioned his intention of leaving the coach at Monkhampton?'

'I don't think I did. As a matter of fact...'

'You were observing the pretty young lady who booked No. 5, the next seat to ours. Ah! Yes, my friend, I saw you. And that is why when I was on the point of taking seats No. 13 and 14—which are in the middle and as well sheltered as it is possible to be—you rudely pushed yourself forward and said that 3 and 4 would be better.'

'Really, Poirot,' I said, blushing.

'Auburn hair—always the auburn hair!'

'At any rate, she was more worth looking at than an odd young man.'

'That depends upon the point of view. To me, the young man was interesting.'

Something rather significant in Poirot's tone made me look at him quickly. 'Why? What do you mean?'

'Oh, do not excite yourself. Shall I say that he interested me because he was trying to grow a moustache and as yet the result is poor.' Poirot stroked his own magnificent moustache tenderly. 'It is an art,' he murmured, 'the growing of the moustache! I have sympathy for all who attempt it.'

It is always difficult with Poirot to know when he is serious and when he is merely amusing himself at one's expense. I judged it safest to say no more.

The following morning dawned bright and sunny. A

really glorious day! Poirot, however, was taking no chances. He wore a woolly waistcoat, a mackintosh, a heavy overcoat, and two mufflers, in addition to wearing his thickest suit. He also swallowed two tablets of 'Anti-grippe' before starting and packed a further supply.

We took a couple of small suitcases with us. The pretty girl we had noticed the day before had a small suitcase, and so did the young man whom I gathered to have been the object of Poirot's sympathy. Otherwise, there was no luggage. The four pieces were stowed away by the driver, and we all took our places.

Poirot, rather maliciously, I thought, assigned me the outside place as 'I had the mania for the fresh air' and himself occupied the seat next to our fair neighbour. Presently, however, he made amends. The man in seat 6 was a noisy fellow, inclined to be facetious and boisterous, and Poirot asked the girl in a low voice if she would like to change seats with him. She agreed gratefully, and the change having been effected, she entered into conversation with us and we were soon all three chattering together merrily.

She was evidently quite young, not more than nineteen, and as ingenuous as a child. She soon confided to us the reason for her trip. She was going, it seemed, on business for her aunt who kept a most interesting antique shop in Ebermouth.

This aunt had been left in very reduced circumstances on the death of her father and had used her small capital and a houseful of beautiful things which her father had left her to start in business. She had been extremely successful and had made quite a name for herself in the trade. This girl, Mary Durrant, had come to be with her aunt and learn the business and was very excited about it—much preferring it to the other alternative—becoming a nursery governess or companion.

Poirot nodded interest and approval to all this.

'Mademoiselle will be successful, I am sure,' he said gallantly. 'But I will give her a little word of advice. Do not be too trusting, mademoiselle. Everywhere in the world there are rogues and vagabonds, even it may be on this very coach of ours. One should always be on the guard, suspicious!'

She stared at him open-mouthed, and he nodded sapiently.

'But yes, it is as I say. Who knows? Even I who speak to you may be a malefactor of the worst description.'

And he twinkled more than ever at her surprised face.

We stopped for lunch at Monkhampton, and, after a few words with the waiter, Poirot managed to secure us a small table for three close by the window. Outside, in a big courtyard, about twenty char-à-bancs were parked—char-à-bancs which had come from all over the country. The hotel dining-room was full, and the noise was rather considerable.

'One can have altogether too much of the holiday spirit,' I said with a grimace.

Mary Durrant agreed. 'Ebermouth is quite spoiled in the summers nowadays. My aunt says it used to be quite different. Now one can hardly get along the pavements for the crowd.'

'But it is good for business, mademoiselle.'

'Not for ours particularly. We sell only rare and valuable things. We do not go in for cheap bric-a-brac. My aunt has clients all over England. If they want a particular period table or chair, or a certain piece of china, they write to her, and, sooner or later, she gets it for them. That is what has happened in this case.'

We looked interested and she went on to explain. A certain American gentleman, Mr J. Baker Wood, was a connoisseur and collector of miniatures. A very valuable set of miniatures had recently come into the market, and Miss Elizabeth Penn—Mary's aunt—had purchased them. She had written to Mr Wood describing the miniatures and naming a price. He had replied at once, saying that he was prepared to purchase if the miniatures were as represented and asking that someone should be sent with them for him to see where he was staying at Charlock Bay. Miss Durrant had accordingly been despatched, acting as representative for the firm.

'They're lovely things, of course,' she said. 'But I can't imagine anyone paying all that money for them. Five hundred pounds! Just think of it! They're by Cosway. Is it Cosway I mean? I get so mixed up in these things.'

Poirot smiled. 'You are not yet experienced, eh, mademoiselle?'

'I've had no training,' said Mary ruefully. 'We weren't brought up to know about old things. It's a lot to learn.'

She sighed. Then suddenly, I saw her eyes widen in surprise. She was sitting facing the window, and her glance now was directed out of that window, into the courtyard. With a hurried word, she rose from her seat and almost ran out of the room. She returned in a few moments, breathless and apologetic.

'I'm so sorry rushing off like that. But I thought I saw a man taking my suitcase out of the coach. I went flying after him, and it turned out to be his own. It's one almost exactly like mine. I felt like such a fool. It looked as though I were accusing him of stealing it.'

She laughed at the idea.

Poirot, however, did not laugh. 'What man was it, mademoiselle? Describe him to me.'

'He had on a brown suit. A thin weedy young man with a very indeterminate moustache.'

'Aha,' said Poirot. 'Our friend of yesterday, Hastings. You know this young man, mademoiselle? You have seen him before?'

'No, never. Why?'

'Nothing. It is rather curious—that is all.'

He relapsed into silence and took no further part in the conversation until something Mary Durrant said caught his attention.

'Eh, mademoiselle, what is that you say?'

'I said that on my return journey I should have to be careful of "malefactors", as you call them. I believe Mr Wood always pays for things in cash. If I have five hundred pounds in notes on me, I shall be worth some malefactor's attention.'

She laughed but Poirot did not respond. Instead, he asked her what hotel she proposed to stay at in Charlock Bay.

'The Anchor Hotel. It is small and not expensive, but quite good.'

'So!' said Poirot. 'The Anchor Hotel. Precisely where Hastings here has made up his mind to stay. How odd!'

He twinkled at me.

'You are staying long in Charlock Bay?' asked Mary.

'One night only. I have business there. You could not guess, I am sure, what my profession is, mademoiselle?'

I saw Mary consider several possibilities and reject them—probably from a feeling of caution. At last, she hazarded the suggestion that Poirot was a conjurer. He was vastly entertained.

'Ah! But it is an idea that! You think I take the rabbits out of the hat? No, mademoiselle. Me, I am the opposite of a conjurer. The conjurer, he makes things disappear. Me, I make things that have disappeared, reappear.'

He leaned forward dramatically so as to give the words full effect. 'It is a secret, mademoiselle, but I will tell you, I am a detective!' He leaned back in his chair pleased with the effect he had created. Mary Durrant stared at him spellbound. But any further conversation was barred for the braying of various horns outside announced that the road monsters were ready to proceed.

As Poirot and I went out together I commented on the charm of our luncheon companion. Poirot agreed.

'Yes, she is charming. But, also rather silly?'

'Silly?'

'Do not be outraged. A girl may be beautiful and have auburn hair and yet be silly. It is the height of foolishness to take two strangers into her confidence as she has done.'

'Well, she could see we were all right.'

'That is imbecile, what you say, my friend. Anyone who knows his job—naturally he will appear "all right". That little one she talked of being careful when she would have five hundred pounds in money with her. But she has five hundred pounds with her now.'

'In miniatures.'

'Exactly. In miniatures. And between one and the other, there is no great difference, *mon ami*.'

'But no one knew about them except us.'

'And the waiter and the people at the next table. And, doubtless, several people in Ebermouth! Mademoiselle Durrant, she is charming, but, if I were Miss Elizabeth Penn, I would first of all instruct my new assistant in the common sense.' He paused and then said in a different voice: 'You know, my friend, it would be the easiest thing in the world to remove a suitcase from one of those char-à-bancs while we were all at luncheon.'

'Oh, come, Poirot, somebody will be sure to see.'

'And what would they see? Somebody removing his luggage. It would be done in an open and above-board manner, and it would be nobody's business to interfere.'

'Do you mean—Poirot, are you hinting—But that fellow in the brown suit—it was his own suitcase?'

Poirot frowned. 'So it seems. All the same, it is curious, Hastings, that he should have not removed his suitcase before, when the car first arrived. He has not lunched here, you notice.'

'If Miss Durrant hadn't been sitting opposite the window, she wouldn't have seen him,' I said slowly.

'And since it was his own suitcase, that would not have mattered,' said Poirot. 'So let us dismiss it from our thoughts, *mon ami.*'

Nevertheless, when we had resumed our places and were speeding along once more, he took the opportunity of giving Mary Durrant a further lecture on the dangers of indiscretion which she received meekly enough but with the air of thinking it all rather a joke.

We arrived at Charlock Bay at four o'clock and were fortunate enough to be able to get rooms at the Anchor

Hotel—a charming old-world inn in one of the side streets.

Poirot had just unpacked a few necessaries and was applying a little cosmetic to his moustache preparatory to going out to call upon Joseph Aarons when there came a frenzied knocking at the door. I called 'Come in,' and, to my utter amazement, Mary Durrant appeared, her face white and large tears standing in her eyes.

'I do beg your pardon—but—but the most awful thing has happened. And you did say you were a detective?' This to Poirot.

'What has happened, mademoiselle?'

'I opened my suitcase. The miniatures were in a crocodile despatch case—locked, of course. Now, look!'

She held out a small square crocodile-covered case. The lid hung loose. Poirot took it from her. The case had been forced; great strength must have been used. The marks were plain enough. Poirot examined it and nodded.

'The miniatures?' he asked, though we both knew the answer well enough.

'Gone. They've been stolen. Oh, what shall I do?'

'Don't worry,' I said. 'My friend is Hercule Poirot. You must have heard of him. He'll get them back for you if anyone can.'

'Monsieur Poirot. The great Monsieur Poirot.'

Poirot was vain enough to be pleased at the obvious reverence in her voice. 'Yes, my child,' he said. 'It is I, myself. And you can leave your little affair in my hands. I will do all that can be done. But I fear—I much fear—that it will be too late. Tell me, was the lock of your suitcase forced also?'

She shook her head.

'Let me see it, please.'

We went together to her room, and Poirot examined the suitcase closely. It had obviously been opened with a key.

'Which is simple enough. These suitcase locks are all much of the same pattern. *Eh bien*, we must ring up the police and we must also get in touch with Mr Baker Wood as soon as possible. I will attend to that myself.'

I went with him and asked what he meant by saying it might be too late. '*Mon cher*, I said today that I was the opposite of the conjurer—that I make the disappearing things reappear—but suppose someone has been beforehand with me. You do not understand? You will in a minute.'

He disappeared into the telephone box. He came out five minutes later looking very grave. 'It is as I feared. A lady called upon Mr Wood with the miniatures half an hour ago. She represented herself as coming from Miss Elizabeth Penn. He was delighted with the miniatures and paid for them forthwith.'

'Half an hour ago—before we arrived here.'

Poirot smiled rather enigmatically. 'The Speedy cars are quite speedy, but a fast motor from, say, Monkhampton would get here a good hour ahead of them at least.'

'And what do we do now?'

'The good Hastings—always practical. We inform the police, do all we can for Miss Durrant, and—yes, I think decidedly, we have an interview with Mr J. Baker Wood.'

We carried out this programme. Poor Mary Durrant was terribly upset, fearing her aunt would blame her.

'Which she probably will,' observed Poirot, as we set out for the Seaside Hotel where Mr Wood was staying. 'And with perfect justice. The idea of leaving five hundred pounds' worth of valuables in a suitcase and going to lunch! All the same, *mon ami*, there are one or two curious points about the case. That despatch box, for instance, why was it forced?'

'To get out the miniatures.'

'But was not that a foolishness? Say our thief is tampering with the luggage at lunch-time under the pretext of getting out his own. Surely it is much simpler to open the suitcase, transfer the despatch case unopened to his own suitcase, and get away, than to waste the time forcing the lock?'

'He had to make sure the miniatures were inside.'

Poirot did not look convinced, but, as we were just being shown into Mr Wood's suite, we had no time for more discussion.

I took an immediate dislike to Mr Baker Wood.

He was a large vulgar man, very much overdressed and wearing a diamond solitaire ring. He was blustering and noisy.

Of course, he'd not suspected anything amiss. Why should he? The woman said she had the miniatures all right. Very fine specimens, too! Had he the numbers of the notes? No, he hadn't. And who was Mr— er—Poirot, anyway, to come asking him all these questions?

'I will not ask you anything more, monsieur, except for one thing. A description of the woman who called upon you. Was she young and pretty?'

'No, sir, she was not. Most emphatically not. A tall

82

woman, middle-aged, grey hair, blotchy complexion and a budding moustache. A siren? Not on your life.'

'Poirot,' I cried, as we took our departure. 'A moustache. Did you hear?'

'I have the use of my ears, thank you, Hastings!'

'But what a very unpleasant man.'

'He has not the charming manner, no.'

'Well, we ought to get the thief all right,' I remarked. 'We can identify him.'

'You are of such a naïve simplicity, Hastings. Do you not know that there is such a thing as an alibi?'

'You think he will have an alibi?'

Poirot replied unexpectedly: 'I sincerely hope so.'

'The trouble with you is,' I said, 'that you like a thing to be difficult.'

'Quite right, *mon ami*. I do not like—how do you say it—the bird who sits!'

Poirot's prophecy was fully justified. Our travelling companion in the brown suit turned out to be a Mr Norton Kane. He had gone straight to the George Hotel at Monkhampton and had been there during the afternoon. The only evidence against him was that of Miss Durrant who declared that she had seen him getting out his luggage from the car while we were at lunch.

'Which in itself is not a suspicious act,' said Poirot meditatively.

After that remark, he lapsed into silence and refused to discuss the matter any further, saying when I pressed him, that he was thinking of moustaches in general, and that I should be well advised to do the same.

I discovered, however, that he had asked Joseph Aarons—with whom he spent the evening—to give him every detail possible about Mr Baker Wood. As both men were staying at the same hotel, there was a chance of gleaning some stray crumbs of information. Whatever Poirot learned, he kept to himself, however.

Mary Durrant, after various interviews with the police, had returned to Ebermouth by an early morning train. We lunched with Joseph Aarons, and after lunch, Poirot announced to me that he had settled the theatrical agent's problem satisfactorily, and that we could return to Ebermouth as soon as we liked. 'But not by road, *mon ami*; we go by rail this time.'

'Are you afraid of having your pocket picked, or of meeting another damsel in distress?'

'Both those affairs, Hastings, might happen to me on the train. No, I am in haste to be back in Ebermouth, because I want to proceed with our case.'

'Our case?'

'But, yes, my friend. Mademoiselle Durrant appealed to me to help her. Because the matter is now in the hands of the police, it does not follow that I am free to wash my hands of it. I came here to oblige an old friend, but it shall never be said of Hercule Poirot that he deserted a stranger in need!' And he drew himself up grandiloquently.

'I think you were interested before that,' I said shrewdly. 'In the office of cars, when you first caught sight of that young man, though what drew your attention to him I don't know.'

'Don't you, Hastings? You should. Well, well, that must remain my little secret.'

We had a short conversation with the police inspector in charge of the case before leaving. He had interviewed Mr Norton Kane, and told Poirot in confidence that the young man's manner had not impressed him favourably. He had blustered, denied, and contradicted himself.

'But just how the trick was done, I don't know,' he confessed. 'He could have handed the stuff to a confederate who pushed off at once in a fast car. But that's just theory. We've got to find the car and the confederate and pin the thing down.'

Poirot nodded thoughtfully.

'Do you think that was how it was done?' I asked him, as we were seated in the train.

'No, my friend, that was not how it was done. It was cleverer than that.'

'Won't you tell me?'

'Not yet. You know—it is my weakness—I like to keep my little secrets till the end.'

'Is the end going to be soon?'

'Very soon now.'

We arrived in Ebermouth a little after six and Poirot drove at once to the shop which bore the name 'Elizabeth Penn'. The establishment was closed, but Poirot rang the bell, and presently Mary herself opened the door, and expressed surprise and delight at seeing us.

'Please come in and see my aunt,' she said.

She led us into a back room. An elderly lady came forward to meet us; she had white hair and looked rather like a miniature herself with her pink-and-white skin and her blue eyes. Round her rather bent shoulders she wore a cape of priceless old lace.

'Is this the great Monsieur Poirot?' she asked in a low charming voice. 'Mary has been telling me. I could hardly believe it. And you will really help us in our trouble. You will advise us?'

85

Poirot looked at her for a moment, then bowed.

'Mademoiselle Penn—the effect is charming. But you should really grow a moustache.'

Miss Penn gave a gasp and drew back.

'You were absent from business yesterday, were you not?'

'I was here in the morning. Later I had a bad headache and went directly home.'

'Not home, mademoiselle. For your headache you tried the change of air, did you not? The air of Charlock Bay is very bracing, I believe.'

He took me by the arm and drew me towards the door. He paused there and spoke over his shoulder.

'You comprehend, I know everything. This little— farce—it must cease.'

There was a menace in his tone. Miss Penn, her face ghastly white, nodded mutely. Poirot turned to the girl.

'Mademoiselle,' he said gently, 'you are young and charming. But participating in these little affairs will lead to that youth and charm being hidden behind prison walls—and I, Hercule Poirot, tell you that that will be a pity.'

Then he stepped out into the street and I followed him, bewildered.

'From the first, *mon ami*, I was interested. When that young man booked his place as far as Monkhampton only, I saw the girl's attention suddenly riveted on him. Now why? He was not of the type to make a woman look at him for himself alone. When we started on the coach, I had a feeling that something would happen. Who saw the young man tampering with the luggage? Mademoiselle and mademoiselle only, and remember she chose that seat—a seat facing the window—a most unfeminine choice.

'And then she comes to us with the tale of robbery—the despatch box forced which makes not the common sense, as I told you at the time.

'And what is the result of it all? Mr Baker Wood has paid over good money for stolen goods. The miniatures will be returned to Miss Penn. She will sell them and will have made a thousand pounds instead of five hundred. I make the discreet inquiries and learn that her business is in a bad state—touch and go. I say to myself—the aunt and niece are in this together.'

'Then you never suspected Norton Kane?'

'*Mon ami*! With that moustache? A criminal is either clean shaven or he has a proper moustache that can be removed at will. But what an opportunity for the clever Miss Penn—a shrinking elderly lady with a pink-and-white complexion as we saw her. But if she holds herself erect, wears large boots, alters her complexion with a few unseemly blotches and—crowning touch—adds a few sparse hairs to her upper lip. What then? A masculine woman, says Mr Wood and "a man in disguise" say we at once.'

'She really went to Charlock yesterday?'

'Assuredly. The train, as you may remember telling me, left here at eleven and got to Charlock Bay at two o'clock. Then the return train is even quicker—the one we came by. It leaves Charlock at four-five and gets here at six-fifteen. Naturally, the miniatures were never in the despatch case at all. That was artistically forced before being packed. Mademoiselle Mary has only to find a couple of mugs who will be sympathetic to her charm and champion beauty in distress. But one of the mugs was no mug—he was Hercule Poirot!'

I hardly liked the inference. I said hurriedly: 'Then when you said you were helping a stranger, you were wilfully deceiving me. That's exactly what you were doing.'

'Never do I deceive you, Hastings. I only permit you to deceive yourself. I was referring to Mr Baker Wood—a stranger to these shores.' His face darkened. 'Ah! When I think of that imposition, that iniquitous over-charge, the same fare single to Charlock as return, my blood boils to protect the visitor! Not a pleasant man, Mr Baker Wood, not, as you would say, sympathetic. But a visitor! And we visitors, Hastings, must stand together. Me, I am all for the visitors!'

# The Hound of Death

It was from William P. Ryan, American newspaper correspondent, that I first heard of the affair. I was dining with him in London on the eve of his return to New York and happened to mention that on the morrow I was going down to Folbridge.

He looked up and said sharply: 'Folbridge, Cornwall?'

Now only about one person in a thousand knows that there is a Folbridge in Cornwall. They always take it for granted that the Folbridge, Hampshire, is meant. So Ryan's knowledge aroused my curiosity.

'Yes,' I said. 'Do you know it?'

He merely replied that he was darned. He then asked if I happened to know a house called Trearne down there.

My interest increased.

'Very well indeed. In fact, it's to Trearne I'm going. It's my sister's house.'

'Well,' said William P. Ryan. 'If that doesn't beat the band!'

I suggested that he should cease making cryptic remarks and explain himself.

'Well,' he said. 'To do that I shall have to go back to an experience of mine at the beginning of the war.'

I sighed. The events which I am relating took place in 1921. To be reminded of the war was the last thing any man wanted. We were, thank God, beginning to forget . . . Besides, William P. Ryan on his war experiences was apt, as I knew, to be unbelievably long-winded.

But there was no stopping him now.

'At the start of the war, as I dare say you know, I was in Belgium for my paper—moving about some. Well, there's a little village—I'll call it X. A one horse place if there ever was one, but there's quite a big convent there. Nuns in white what do you call 'em—I don't know the name of the order. Anyway, it doesn't matter. Well, this little burgh was right in the way of the German advance. The Uhlans arrived—'

I shifted uneasily. William P. Ryan lifted a hand reassuringly.

'It's all right,' he said. 'This isn't a German atrocity story. It might have been, perhaps, but it isn't. As a matter of fact, the boot's on the other leg. The Germans made for that convent—they got there and the whole thing blew up.'

'Oh!' I said, rather startled.

'Odd business, wasn't it? Of course, off hand, I should say the Germans had been celebrating and had monkeyed round with their own explosives. But it seems they hadn't anything of that kind with them. They weren't the high explosive johnnies. Well, then, I ask you, what should a pack of nuns know about high explosive? Some nuns, I should say!'

'It is odd,' I agreed.

'I was interested in hearing the peasants' account of the matter. They'd got it all cut and dried. According to them it was a slap-up one hundred per cent efficient first-class modern miracle. It seems one of the nuns had got something of a reputation—a budding saint—went into trances and saw visions. And according to them she worked the stunt. She called down the lightning to blast the impious German—and it blasted him all right—and everything else within range. A pretty efficient miracle, that!

'I never really got at the truth of the matter—hadn't time. But miracles were all the rage just then—angels at Mons and all that. I wrote up the thing, put in a bit of sob stuff, and pulled the religious stop out well, and sent it to my paper. It went down very well in the States. They were liking that kind of thing just then.

'But (I don't know if you'll understand this) in writing, I got kinda interested. I felt I'd like to know what really had happened. There was nothing to see at the spot itself. Two walls still left standing, and on one of them was a black powder mark that was the exact shape of a great hound. The peasants round about were scared to death of that mark. They called it the Hound of Death and they wouldn't pass that way after dark.

'Superstition's always interesting. I felt I'd like to see the lady who worked the stunt. She hadn't perished, it seemed. She'd gone to England with a batch of other refugees. I took the trouble to trace her. I found she'd been sent to Trearne, Folbridge, Cornwall.'

I nodded.

'My sister took in a lot of Belgian refugees the beginning of the war. About twenty.'

'Well, I always meant, if I had time, to look up the lady. I wanted to hear her own account of the disaster. Then, what with being busy and one thing and another, it slipped my memory. Cornwall's a bit out of the way anyhow. In fact, I'd forgotten the whole thing till your mentioning Folbridge just now brought it back.'

'I must ask my sister,' I said. 'She may have heard something about it. Of course, the Belgians have all been repatriated long ago.'

'Naturally. All the same, in case your sister does know anything I'll be glad if you'd pass it on to me.'

'Of course I will,' I said heartily.

And that was that.

It was the second day after my arrival at Trearne that the story recurred to me. My sister and I were having tea on the terrace.

'Kitty,' I said, 'didn't you have a nun among your Belgians?'

'You don't mean Sister Marie Angelique, do you?'

'Possibly I do,' I said cautiously. 'Tell me about her.'

'Oh! my dear, she was the most uncanny creature. She's still here, you know.'

'What? In the house?'

'No, no, in the village. Dr Rose—you remember Dr Rose?'

I shook my head.

'I remember an old man of about eighty-three.'

'Dr Laird. Oh! he died. Dr Rose has only been here a few years. He's quite young and very keen on new ideas. He took the most enormous interest in Sister Marie Angelique. She has hallucinations and things, you know, and apparently is most frightfully interesting from a medical point of view. Poor thing, she'd nowhere to go—and really was in my opinion quite potty—only impressive, if you know what I mean—well, as I say, she'd nowhere to go, and Dr Rose very kindly fixed her up in the village. I believe he's writing a monograph or whatever it is that doctors write, about her.'

She paused and then said:

'But what do you know about her?'

'I heard a rather curious story.'

I passed on the story as I had received it from Ryan. Kitty was very much interested.

'She looks the sort of person who could blast you—if you know what I mean,' she said.

'I really think,' I said, my curiosity heightened, 'that I must see this young woman.'

'Do. I'd like to know what you think of her. Go and see Dr Rose first. Why not walk down to the village after tea?'

I accepted the suggestion.

I found Dr Rose at home and introduced myself. He seemed a pleasant young man, yet there was something about his personality that rather repelled me. It was too forceful to be altogether agreeable.

The moment I mentioned Sister Marie Angelique he stiffened to attention. He was evidently keenly interested. I gave him Ryan's account of the matter.

'Ah!' he said thoughtfully. 'That explains a great deal.'

He looked up quickly at me and went on.

'The case is really an extraordinarily interesting one. The woman arrived here having evidently suffered some severe mental shock. She was in a state of great mental excitement also. She was given to hallucinations of a most startling character. Her personality is most unusual. Perhaps you would like to come with me and call upon her. She is really well worth seeing.'

I agreed readily.

We set out together. Our objective was a small cottage on the outskirts of the village. Folbridge is a most picturesque place. It lies at the mouth of the river Fol mostly on the east bank, the west bank is too precipitous for building, though a few cottages do cling to the cliffside there. The doctor's own cottage was perched on the extreme edge of the cliff on the west side. From it you looked down on the big waves lashing against the black rocks.

The little cottage to which we were now proceeding lay inland out of sight of the sea.

'The district nurse lives here,' explained Dr Rose. 'I have arranged for Sister Marie Angelique to board with her. It is just as well that she should be under skilled supervision.'

'Is she quite normal in her manner?' I asked curiously.

'You can judge for yourself in a minute,' he replied, smiling.

The district nurse, a dumpy pleasant little body, was just setting out on her bicycle when we arrived.

'Good evening, nurse, how's your patient?' called out the doctor.

'She's much as usual, doctor. Just sitting there with her hands folded and her mind far away. Often enough she'll not answer when I speak to her, though for the matter of that it's little enough English she understands even now.'

Rose nodded, and as the nurse bicycled away, he went up to the cottage door, rapped sharply and entered.

Sister Marie Angelique was lying in a long chair near the window. She turned her head as we entered.

It was a strange face—pale, transparent looking, with enormous eyes. There seemed to be an infinitude of tragedy in those eyes.

'Good evening, my sister,' said the doctor in French.

'Good evening, M. le docteur.'

'Permit me to introduce a friend, Mr Anstruther.'

I bowed and she inclined her head with a faint smile.

'And how are you today?' inquired the doctor, sitting down beside her.

'I am much the same as usual.' She paused and then went on. 'Nothing seems real to me. Are they days that pass—or months—or years? I hardly know. Only my dreams seem real to me.'

'You still dream a lot, then?'

'Always—always—and, you understand?—the dreams seem more real than life.'

'You dream of your own country—of Belgium?'

She shook her head.

'No. I dream of a country that never existed—never. But you know this, M. le docteur. I have told you many times.' She stopped and then said abruptly: 'But perhaps this gentleman is also a doctor—a doctor perhaps for the diseases of the brain?'

'No, no.' Rose said reassuring, but as he smiled I noticed how extraordinarily pointed his canine teeth were, and it occurred to me that there was something wolf-like about the man. He went on:

'I thought you might be interested to meet Mr

Anstruther. He knows something of Belgium. He has lately been hearing news of your convent.'

Her eyes turned to me. A faint flush crept into her cheeks.

'It's nothing, really,' I hastened to explain. 'But I was dining the other evening with a friend who was describing the ruined walls of the convent to me.'

'So it was ruined!'

It was a soft exclamation, uttered more to herself than to us. Then looking at me once more she asked hesitatingly: 'Tell me, Monsieur, did your friend say how—in what way—it was ruined?'

'It was blown up,' I said, and added: 'The peasants are afraid to pass that way at night.'

'Why are they afraid?'

'Because of a black mark on a ruined wall. They have a superstitious fear of it.'

She leaned forward.

'Tell me, Monsieur—quick—quick—tell me! What is that mark like?'

'It has the shape of a huge hound,' I answered. 'The peasants call it the Hound of Death.'

'Ah!'

A shrill cry burst from her lips.

'It is true then—it is true. All that I remember is true. It is not some black nightmare. It happened! It happened!'

'What happened, my sister?' asked the doctor in a low voice.

She turned to him eagerly.

'*I remembered*. There on the steps, I remembered. I remembered the way of it. I used the power as we used to use it. I stood on the altar steps and I bade them to come no farther. I told them to depart in peace. They would not listen, they came on although I warned them. And so—' She leaned forward and made a curious gesture. 'And so I loosed the Hound of Death on them . . .'

She lay back on her chair shivering all over, her eyes closed.

The doctor rose, fetched a glass from a cupboard, half-filled it with water, added a drop or two from a little bottle which he produced from his pocket, then took the glass to her.

'Drink this,' he said authoritatively.

She obeyed—mechanically as it seemed. Her eyes looked far away as though they contemplated some inner vision of her own.

'But then it is all true,' she said. 'Everything. The City of the Circles, the People of the Crystal—everything. It is all true.'

'It would seem so,' said Rose.

His voice was low and soothing, clearly designed to encourage and not to disturb her train of thought.

'Tell me about the City,' he said. 'The City of Circles, I think you said?'

She answered absently and mechanically.

'Yes—there were three circles. The first circle for the chosen, the second for the priestesses and the outer circle for the priests.'

'And in the centre?'

She drew her breath sharply and her voice sank to a tone of indescribable awe.

'The House of the Crystal . . .'

As she breathed the words, her right hand went to her forehead and her finger traced some figure there.

Her figure seemed to grow more rigid, her eyes closed, she swayed a little—then suddenly she sat upright with a jerk, as though she had suddenly awakened.

'What is it?' she said confusedly. 'What have I been saying?'

'It is nothing,' said Rose. 'You are tired. You want to rest. We will leave you.'

She seemed a little dazed as we took our departure.

'Well,' said Rose when we were outside. 'What do you think of it?'

He shot a sharp glance sideways at me.

'I suppose her mind must be totally unhinged,' I said slowly.

'It struck you like that?'

'No—as a matter of fact, she was—well, curiously convincing. When listening to her I had the impression that she actually had done what she claimed to do— worked a kind of gigantic miracle. Her belief that she did so seems genuine enough. That is why—'

'That is why you say her mind must be unhinged. Quite so. But now approach the matter from another angle. Supposing that she did actually work that miracle—supposing that she did, personally, destroy a building and several hundred human beings.'

'By the mere exercise of will?' I said with a smile.

'I should not put it quite like that. You will agree that one person could destroy a multitude by touching a switch which controlled a system of mines.'

'Yes, but that is mechanical.'

'True, that is mechanical, but it is, in essence, the harnessing and controlling of natural forces. The thunder-storm and the power house are, fundamentally, the same thing.'

'Yes, but to control the thunderstorm we have to use mechanical means.'

Rose smiled.

'I am going off at a tangent now. There is a substance called wintergreen. It occurs in nature in vegetable form. It can also be built up by man synthetically and chemically in the laboratory.'

'Well?'

'My point is that there are often two ways of arriving at the same result. Ours is, admittedly, the synthetic way. There might be another. The extraordinary results arrived at by Indian fakirs for instance, cannot be explained away in any easy fashion. The things we call supernatural are not necessarily supernatural at all. An electric flashlight would be supernatural to a savage. The supernatural is only the natural of which the laws are not yet understood.'

'You mean?' I asked, fascinated.

'That I cannot entirely dismiss the possibility that a human being *might* be able to tap some vast destructive force and use it to further his or her ends. The means by which this was accomplished might seem to us supernatural—but would not be so in reality.'

I stared at him.

He laughed.

'It's a speculation, that's all,' he said lightly. 'Tell me, did you notice a gesture she made when she mentioned the House of the Crystal?'

'She put her hand to her forehead.'

'Exactly. And traced a circle there. Very much as a Catholic makes the sign of the cross. Now, I will tell you something rather interesting, Mr Anstruther. The word crystal having occurred so often in my patient's rambling, I tried an experiment. I borrowed a crystal from someone and produced it unexpectedly one day to test my patient's reaction to it.'

'Well?'

'Well, the result was very curious and suggestive. Her whole body stiffened. She stared at it as though unable to believe her eyes. Then she slid to her knees in front of it, murmured a few words—and fainted.'

'What were the few words?'

'Very curious ones. She said: "*The Crystal! Then the Faith still lives!*"'

'Extraordinary!'

'Suggestive, is it not? Now the next curious thing. When she came round from her faint she had forgotten the whole thing. I showed her the crystal and asked her if she knew what it was. She replied that she supposed it was a crystal such as fortune tellers used. I asked her if she had ever seen one before? She replied: "Never, M. le docteur." But I saw a puzzled look in her eyes. "What troubles you, my sister?" I asked. She replied: "Because it is so strange. I have never seen a crystal before and yet—it seems to me that I know it well. There is something—if only I could remember . . ." The effort at memory was obviously so distressing to her that I forbade her to think any more. That was two weeks ago. I have purposely been biding my time. Tomorrow, I shall proceed to a further experiment.'

'With the crystal?'

'With the crystal. I shall get her to gaze into it. I think the result ought to be interesting.'

'What do you expect to get hold of?' I asked curiously.

The words were idle ones but they had an unlooked-for result. Rose stiffened, flushed, and his manner when he spoke changed insensibly. It was more formal, more professional.

'Light on certain mental disorders imperfectly understood. Sister Marie Angelique is a most interesting study.'

So Rose's interest was purely professional? I wondered.

'Do you mind if I come along too?' I asked.

It may have been my fancy, but I thought he hesitated before he replied. I had a sudden intuition that he did not want me.

'Certainly. I can see no objection.'

He added: 'I suppose you're not going to be down here very long?'

'Only till the day after tomorrow.'

I fancied that the answer pleased him. His brow cleared and he began talking of some recent experiments carried out on guinea pigs.

I met the doctor by appointment the following afternoon, and we went together to Sister Marie Angelique. Today, the doctor was all geniality. He was anxious, I thought, to efface the impression he had made the day before.

'You must not take what I said too seriously,' he observed, laughing. 'I shouldn't like you to believe me a dabbler in occult sciences. The worst of me is I have an infernal weakness for making out a case.'

'Really?'

'Yes, and the more fantastic it is, the better I like it.'

He laughed as a man laughs at an amusing weakness.

When we arrived at the cottage, the district nurse had something she wanted to consult Rose about, so I was left with Sister Marie Angelique.

I saw her scrutinizing me closely. Presently she spoke.

'The good nurse here, she tells me that you are the brother of the kind lady at the big house where I was brought when I came from Belgium?'

'Yes,' I said.

'She was very kind to me. She is good.'

She was silent, as though following out some train of thought. Then she said:

'M. le docteur, he too is a good man?'

I was a little embarrassed.

'Why, yes. I mean—I think so.'

'Ah!' She paused and then said: 'Certainly he has been very kind to me.'

'I'm sure he has.'

She looked up at me sharply.

'Monsieur—you—you who speak to me now—do you believe that I am mad?'

'Why, my sister, such an idea never—'

She shook her head slowly—interrupting my protest.

'Am I mad? I do not know—the things I remember—the things I forget . . .'

She sighed, and at that moment Rose entered the room.

He greeted her cheerily and explained what he wanted her to do.

'Certain people, you see, have a gift for seeing things in a crystal. I fancy you might have such a gift, my sister.'

She looked distressed.

'No, no, I cannot do that. To try to read the future—that is sinful.'

Rose was taken aback. It was the nun's point of view for which he had not allowed. He changed his ground cleverly.

'One should not look into the future. You are quite right. But to look into the past—that is different.'

'The past?'

'Yes—there are many strange things in the past. Flashes come back to one—they are seen for a moment—then gone again. Do not seek to see anything in the crystal since that is not allowed you. Just take it in your hands—so. Look into it—look deep. Yes—deeper—deeper still. You remember, do you not? You remember. You hear me speaking to you. You can answer my questions. Can you not hear me?'

Sister Marie Angelique had taken the crystal as bidden, handling it with a curious reverence. Then, as she gazed into it, her eyes became blank and unseeing, her head drooped. She seemed to sleep.

Gently the doctor took the crystal from her and put it on the table. He raised the corner of her eyelid. Then he came and sat by me.

'We must wait till she wakes. It won't be long, I fancy.'

He was right. At the end of five minutes, Sister Marie Angelique stirred. Her eyes opened dreamily. 'Where am I?'

'You are here—at home. You have had a little sleep. You have dreamt, have you not?'

She nodded.

'Yes, I have dreamt.'

'You have dreamt of the Crystal?'

'Yes.'

'Tell us about it.'

'You will think me mad, M. le docteur. For see you, in my dream, the Crystal was a holy emblem. I even figured to myself a second Christ, a Teacher of the Crystal who died for his faith, his followers hunted down—persecuted . . . But the faith endured.

'The faith endured?'

'Yes—for fifteen thousand full moons—I mean, for fifteen thousand years.'

'How long was a full moon?'

'Thirteen ordinary moons. Yes, it was in the fifteen thousandth full moon—of course, I was a Priestess of the Fifth Sign in the House of the Crystal. It was in the first days of the coming of the Sixth Sign . . .'

Her brows drew together, a look of fear passed over her face.

'Too soon,' she murmured. 'Too soon. A mistake . . . Ah! yes, I remember! The Sixth Sign!'

She half sprang to her feet, then dropped back, passing her hand over her face and murmuring:

'But what am I saying? I am raving. These things never happened.'

'Now don't distress yourself.'

But she was looking at him in anguished perplexity.

'M. le docteur, I do not understand. Why should I have these dreams—these fancies? I was only sixteen when I entered the religious life. I have never travelled. Yet I dream of cities, of strange people, of strange customs. Why?' She pressed both hands to her head.

'Have you ever been hypnotized, my sister? Or been in a state of trance?'

'I have never been hypnotized, M. le docteur. For the

other, when at prayer in the chapel, my spirit has often been caught up from my body, and I have been as one dead for many hours. It was undoubtedly a blessed state, the Reverend Mother said—a state of grace. Ah! yes,' she caught her breath. '*I remember, we too called it a state of grace.*'

'I would like to try an experiment, my sister.' Rose spoke in a matter-of-fact voice. 'It may dispel those painful half-recollections. I will ask you to gaze once more in the crystal. I will then say a certain word to you. You will answer with another. We will continue in this way until you become tired. Concentrate your thoughts on the crystal, not upon the words.'

As I once more unwrapped the crystal and gave it into Sister Marie Angelique's hands, I noticed the reverent way her hands touched it. Reposing on the black velvet, it lay between her slim palms. Her wonderful deep eyes gazed into it. There was a short silence, and then the doctor said: '*Hound.*'

Immediately Sister Marie Angelique answered '*Death.*'

I do not propose to give a full account of the experiment. Many unimportant and meaningless words were purposely introduced by the doctor. Other words he repeated several times, sometimes getting the same answer to them, sometimes a different one.

That evening in the doctor's little cottage on the cliffs we discussed the result of the experiment.

He cleared his throat, and drew his note-book closer to him.

'These results are very interesting—very curious. In answer to the words "Sixth Sign," we get variously

*Destruction, Purple, Hound, Power*, then again *Destruction*, and finally *Power*. Later, as you may have noticed, I reversed the method, with the following results. In answer to *Destruction*, I get *Hound*; to *Purple, Power*; to *Hound, Death*, again, and to *Power, Hound*. That all holds together, but on a second repetition of *Destruction*, I get *Sea*, which appears utterly irrelevant. To the words "Fifth Sign," I get *Blue, Thoughts, Bird, Blue* again, and finally the rather suggestive phrase *Opening of mind to mind*. From the fact that "Fourth Sign" elicits the word *Yellow*, and later *Light*, and that "First Sign" is answered by *Blood*, I deduce that each Sign had a particular colour, and possibly a particular symbol, that of the Fifth Sign being a *bird*, and that of the Sixth a *hound*. However, I surmise that the Fifth Sign represented what is familiarly known as telepathy—the opening of mind to mind. The Sixth Sign undoubtedly stands for the Power of Destruction.'

'What is the meaning of *Sea*?'

'That I confess I cannot explain. I introduced the word later and got the ordinary answer of *Boat*. To Seventh Sign I got first *Life*, the second time *Love*. To Eighth Sign, I got the answer *None*. I take it therefore that Seven was the sum and number of the signs.'

'But the Seventh was not achieved,' I said on a sudden inspiration. 'Since through the Sixth came *Destruction*!'

'Ah! You think so? But we are taking these—mad ramblings very seriously. They are really only interesting from a medical point of view.'

'Surely they will attract the attention of psychic investigators?'

The doctor's eyes narrowed. 'My dear sir, I have no intention of making them public.'

'Then your interest?'

'Is purely personal. I shall make notes on the case, of course.'

'I see.' But for the first time I felt, like the blind man, that I didn't see at all. I rose to my feet.

'Well, I'll wish you good night, doctor. I'm off to town again tomorrow.'

'Ah!' I fancied there was satisfaction, relief perhaps, behind the exclamation.

'I wish you good luck with your investigations,' I continued lightly. 'Don't loose the Hound of Death on me next time we meet!'

His hand was in mine as I spoke, and I felt the start it gave. He recovered himself quickly. His lips drew back from his long pointed teeth in a smile.

'For a man who loved power, what a power that would be!' he said. 'To hold every human being's life in the hollow of your hand!'

And his smile broadened.

That was the end of my direct connection with the affair.

Later, the doctor's note-book and diary came into my hands. I will reproduce the few scanty entries in it here, though you will understand that it did not really come into my possession until some time afterwards.

*Aug. 5th. Have discovered that by 'the Chosen,' Sister M.A. means those who reproduced the race. Apparently they were held in the highest honour, and exalted above the Priesthood. Contrast this with early Christians.*

*Aug. 7th. Persuaded Sister M.A. to let me hypnotise her.*

*Succeeded in inducing hypnoptic sleep and trance, but no rapport established.*

*Aug. 9th. Have there been civilizations in the past to which ours is as nothing? Strange if it should be so, and I the only man with the clue to it . . .*

*Aug. 12th. Sister M.A. not at all amenable to suggestion when hypnotized. Yet state of trance easily induced. Cannot understand it.*

*Aug. 13th. Sister M.A. mentioned today that in 'state of grace' the 'gate must be closed, lest another should command the body'. Interesting—but baffling.*

*Aug. 18th. So the First Sign is none other than . . . (words erased here) . . . then how many centuries will it take to reach the Sixth? But if there should be a short-cut to Power . . .*

*Aug. 20th. Have arranged for M.A. to come here with Nurse. Have told her it is necessary to keep patient under morphia. Am I mad? Or shall I be the Superman, with the Power of Death in my hands?*

(Here the entries cease.)

It was, I think, on August 29th that I received the letter. It was directed to me, care of my sister-in-law, in a sloping foreign handwriting. I opened it with some curiosity. It ran as follows:

*Cher Monsieur,—I have seen you but twice, but I have felt I could trust you. Whether my dreams are real or not, they have grown clearer of late . . . And, Monsieur, one thing at all events, the Hound of Death is no dream . . . In the days I told you of (whether they are real or not, I do not know) He Who was Guardian of the Crystal revealed the*

*Sixth Sign to the people too soon . . . Evil entered into their hearts. They had the power to slay at will—and they slew without justice—in anger. They were drunk with the lust of Power. When we saw this, We who were yet pure, we knew that once again we should not complete the Circle and come to the Sign of Everlasting Life. He who would have been the next Guardian of the Crystal was bidden to act. That the old might die, and the new, after endless ages, might come again,* he loosed the Hound of Death upon the sea *(being careful not to close the circle), and the sea rose up in the shape of a Hound and swallowed the land utterly . . .*

*Once before I remembered this*—on the altar steps in Belgium . . .

*The Dr Rose, he is of the Brotherhood. He knows the First Sign, and the form of the Second, though its meaning is hidden to all save a chosen few.* He would learn of me the Sixth. *I have withstood him so far—but I grow weak. Monsieur, it is not well that a man should come to power before his time. Many centuries must go by ere the world is ready to have the power of death delivered into its hand . . . I beseech of you, Monsieur, you who love goodness and truth, to help me . . . before it is too late.*

*Your sister in Christ,*
*Marie Angelique*

I let the paper fall. The solid earth beneath me seemed a little less solid than usual. Then I began to rally. The poor woman's belief, genuine enough, had almost affected *me*! One thing was clear. Dr Rose, in his zeal for a case, was grossly abusing his professional standing. I would run down and—

Suddenly I noticed a letter from Kitty amongst my other correspondence. I tore it open.

'Such an awful thing has happened,' I read. 'You remember Dr Rose's little cottage on the cliff? It was swept away by a landslide last night, the doctor and that poor nun, Sister Marie Angelique, were killed. The *debris* on the beach is too awful—all piled up in a fantastic mass—from a distance it looks like a great *hound . . .*'

The letter dropped from my hand.

The other facts may be coincidence. A Mr Rose, whom I discovered to be a wealthy relative of the doctor's, died suddenly that same night—it was said struck by lightning. As far as was known no thunderstorm had occurred in the neighbourhood, but one or two people declared they had heard one peal of thunder. He had an electric burn on him 'of a curious shape'. His will left everything to his nephew, Dr Rose.

Now, supposing that Dr Rose succeeded in obtaining the secret of the Sixth Sign from Sister Marie Angelique. I had always felt him to be an unscrupulous man—he would not shrink at taking his uncle's life if he were sure it could not be brought home to him. But one sentence of Sister Marie Angelique's letter rings in my brain . . . 'being careful not to close the Circle . . .' Dr Rose did not exercise that care—was perhaps unaware of the steps to take, or even of the need for them. So the Force he employed returned, completing its circuit . . .

But of course it is all nonsense! Everything can be accounted for quite naturally. That the doctor believed in Sister Marie Angelique's hallucinations merely proves that *his* mind, too, was slightly unbalanced.

Yet sometimes I dream of a continent under the seas where men once lived and attained to a degree of civilization far ahead of ours . . .

Or did Sister Marie Angelique remember *backwards*—as some say is possible—and is this City of the Circles in the future and not in the past?

Nonsense—of course the whole thing was mere hallucination!

# The Cornish Mystery

'Mrs Pengelley,' announced our landlady, and withdrew discreetly.

Many unlikely people came to consult Poirot, but to my mind, the woman who stood nervously just inside the door, fingering her feather neck-piece, was the most unlikely of all. She was so extraordinarily common-place—a thin, faded woman of about fifty, dressed in a braided coat and skirt, some gold jewellery at her neck, and with her grey hair surmounted by a singularly unbecoming hat. In a country town you pass a hundred Mrs Pengelleys in the street every day.

Poirot came forward and greeted her pleasantly, perceiving her obvious embarrassment.

'Madame! Take a chair, I beg of you. My colleague, Captain Hastings.'

The lady sat down, murmuring uncertainly: 'You are M. Poirot, the detective?'

'At your service, madame.'

But our guest was still tongue-tied. She sighed, twisted her fingers, and grew steadily redder and redder.

'There is something I can do for you, eh, madame?'

'Well, I thought—that is—you see—'

'Proceed, madame, I beg of you—proceed.'

Mrs Pengelley, thus encouraged, took a grip on herself.

'It's this way, M. Poirot—I don't want to have anything to do with the police. No, I wouldn't go to the police for anything! But all the same, I'm sorely troubled about something. And yet I don't know if I ought—' She stopped abruptly.

'Me, I have nothing to do with the police. My investigations are strictly private.'

Mrs Pengelley caught at the word.

'Private—that's what I want. I don't want any talk or fuss, or things in the papers. Wicked it is, the way they write things, until the family could never hold up their heads again. And it isn't as though I was even sure—it's just a dreadful idea that's come to me, and put it out of my head I can't.' She paused for breath. 'And all the time I may be wickedly wronging poor Edward. It's a terrible thought for any wife to have. But you do read of such dreadful things nowadays.'

'Permit me—it is of your husband you speak?'

'Yes.'

'And you suspect him of—what?'

'I don't like even to say it, M. Poirot. But you *do* read of such things happening—and the poor souls suspecting nothing.'

I was beginning to despair of the lady's ever coming to the point, but Poirot's patience was equal to the demand made upon it.

'Speak without fear, madame. Think what joy will be yours if we are able to prove your suspicions unfounded.'

'That's true—anything's better than this wearing

113

uncertainty. Oh, M. Poirot, I'm dreadfully afraid I'm being *poisoned*.'

'What makes you think so?'

Mrs Pengelley, her reticence leaving her, plunged into a full recital more suited to the ears of her medical attendant.

'Pain and sickness after food, eh?' said Poirot thoughtfully. 'You have a doctor attending you, madame? What does he say?'

'He says it's acute gastritis, M. Poirot. But I can see that he's puzzled and uneasy, and he's always altering the medicine, but nothing does any good.'

'You have spoken of your—fears, to him?'

'No, indeed, M. Poirot. It might get about in the town. And perhaps it *is* gastritis. All the same, it's very odd that whenever Edward is away for the weekend, I'm quite all right again. Even Freda notices that—my niece, M. Poirot. And then there's that bottle of weed-killer, never used, the gardener says, and yet it's half-empty.'

She looked appealingly at Poirot. He smiled reassuringly at her, and reached for a pencil and notebook.

'Let us be business-like, madame. Now, then, you and your husband reside—where?'

'Polgarwith, a small market town in Cornwall.'

'You have lived there long?'

'Fourteen years.'

'And your household consists of you and your husband. Any children?'

'No.'

'But a niece, I think you said?'

'Yes, Freda Stanton, the child of my husband's only sister. She has lived with us for the last eight years—that is, until a week ago.'

'Oh, and what happened a week ago?'

'Things hadn't been very pleasant for some time; I don't know what had come over Freda. She was so rude and impertinent, and her temper something shocking, and in the end she flared up one day, and out she walked and took rooms of her own in the town. I've not seen her since. Better leave her to come to her senses, so Mr Radnor says.'

'Who is Mr Radnor?'

Some of Mrs Pengelley's initial embarrassment returned. 'Oh, he's—he's just a friend. Very pleasant young fellow.'

'Anything between him and your niece?'

'Nothing whatever,' said Mrs Pengelley emphatically. Poirot shifted his ground.

'You and your husband are, I presume, in comfortable circumstances?'

'Yes, we're very nicely off.'

'The money, is it yours or your husband's?'

'Oh, it's all Edward's. I've nothing of my own.'

'You see, madame, to be business-like, we must be brutal. We must seek for a motive. Your husband, he would not poison you just *pour passer le temps*! Do you know of any reason why he should wish you out of the way?'

'There's the yellow-haired hussy who works for him,' said Mrs Pengelley, with a flash of temper. 'My husband's a dentist, M. Poirot, and nothing would do but he must have a smart girl, as he said, with bobbed hair and a white overall, to make his appointments and mix his fillings for him. It's come to my ears that there have been fine goings-on, though of course he swears it's all right.'

115

'This bottle of weed-killer, madame, who ordered it?'

'My husband—about a year ago.'

'Your niece, now, has she any money of her own?'

'About fifty pounds a year, I should say. She'd be glad enough to come back and keep house for Edward if I left him.'

'You have contemplated leaving him, then?'

'I don't intend to let him have it all his own way. Women aren't the downtrodden slaves they were in the old days, M. Poirot.'

'I congratulate you on your independent spirit, madame; but let us be practical. You return to Polgarwith today?'

'Yes, I came up by an excursion. Six this morning the train started, and the train goes back at five this afternoon.'

'*Bien*! I have nothing of great moment on hand. I can devote myself to your little affair. Tomorrow I shall be in Polgarwith. Shall we say that Hastings, here, is a distant relative of yours, the son of your second cousin? Me, I am his eccentric foreign friend. In the meantime, eat only what is prepared by your own hands, or under your eye. You have a maid whom you trust?'

'Jessie is a very good girl, I am sure.'

'Till tomorrow then, madame, and be of good courage.'

Poirot bowed the lady out, and returned thoughtfully to his chair. His absorption was not so great, however, that he failed to see two minute strands of feather scarf wrenched off by the lady's agitated fingers. He collected them carefully and consigned them to the wastepaper basket.

'What do you make of the case, Hastings?'

'A nasty business, I should say.'

'Yes, if what the lady suspects be true. But is it? Woe betide any husband who orders a bottle of weed-killer nowadays. If his wife suffers from gastritis, and is inclined to be of a hysterical temperament, the fat is in the fire.'

'You think that is all there is to it?'

'Ah—*voilà*—I do not know, Hastings. But the case interests me—it interests me enormously. For, you see, it has positively no new features. Hence the hysterical theory, and yet Mrs Pengelley did not strike me as being a hysterical woman. Yes, if I mistake not, we have here a very poignant human drama. Tell me, Hastings, what do you consider Mrs Pengelley's feelings towards her husband to be?'

'Loyalty struggling with fear,' I suggested.

'Yet, ordinarily, a woman will accuse anyone in the world—but not her husband. She will stick to her belief in him through thick and thin.'

'The "other woman" complicates the matter.'

'Yes, affection may turn to hate, under the stimulus of jealousy. But hate would take her to the police—not to me. She would want an outcry—a scandal. No, no, let us exercise our little grey cells. Why did she come to me? To have her suspicions proved wrong? Or—to have them *proved right*? Ah, we have here something I do not understand—an unknown factor. Is she a superb actress, our Mrs Pengelley? No, she was genuine, I would swear that she was genuine, and therefore I am interested. Look up the trains to Polgarwith, I pray you.'

The best train of the day was the one-fifty from Paddington which reached Polgarwith just after seven o'clock. The journey was uneventful, and I had to rouse myself from a pleasant nap to alight upon the platform of the bleak little station. We took our bags to the Duchy Hotel, and after a light meal, Poirot suggested our stepping round to pay an after-dinner call on my so-called cousin.

The Pengelleys' house stood a little way back from the road with an old-fashioned cottage garden in front. The smell of stocks and mignonette came sweetly wafted on the evening breeze. It seemed impossible to associate thoughts of violence with this Old World charm. Poirot rang and knocked. As the summons was not answered, he rang again. This time, after a little pause, the door was opened by a dishevelled-looking servant. Her eyes were red, and she was sniffing violently.

'We wish to see Mrs Pengelley,' explained Poirot. 'May we enter?'

The maid stared. Then, with unusual directness, she answered: 'Haven't you heard, then? She's dead. Died this evening—about half an hour ago.'

We stood staring at her, stunned.

'What did she die of?' I asked at last.

'There's some as could tell.' She gave a quick glance over her shoulder. 'If it wasn't that somebody ought to be in the house with the missus, I'd pack my box and go tonight. But I'll not leave her dead with no one to watch by her. It's not my place to say anything, and I'm not going to say anything—but everybody knows. It's all over the town. And if Mr Radnor don't write to the 'Ome Secretary, someone else will. The doctor may say what he likes. Didn't I see the master with my own eyes a-lifting down of the weed-killer from the shelf this

118

very evening? And didn't he jump when he turned round and saw me watching of him? And the missus' gruel there on the table, all ready to take to her? Not another bit of food passes my lips while I am in this house! Not if I dies for it.'

'Where does the doctor live who attended your mistress?'

'Dr Adams. Round the corner in High Street. The second house.'

Poirot turned away abruptly. He was very pale.

'For a girl who was not going to say anything, that girl said a lot,' I remarked dryly.

Poirot struck his clenched hand into his palm.

'An imbecile, a criminal imbecile, that is what I have been, Hastings. I have boasted of my little grey cells, and now I have lost a human life, a life that came to me to be saved. Never did I dream that anything would happen so soon. May the good God forgive me, but I never believed anything would happen at all. Her story seemed to me artificial. Here we are at the doctor's. Let us see what he can tell us.'

Dr Adams was the typical genial red-faced country doctor of fiction. He received us politely enough, but at a hint of our errand, his red face became purple.

'Damned nonsense! Damned nonsense, every word of it! Wasn't I in attendance on the case? Gastritis—gastritis pure and simple. This town's a hotbed of gossip—a lot of scandal-mongering old women get together and invent God knows what. They read these scurrilous rags of newspapers, and nothing will suit them but that someone in their town shall get poisoned too. They see a bottle of weed-killer on a shelf—and hey presto!—away goes their imagination with the bit between its teeth. I know Edward Pengelley—he wouldn't poison his grandmother's dog. And why should he poison his wife? Tell me that?'

'There is one thing, M. le Docteur, that perhaps you do not know.'

And, very briefly, Poirot outlined the main facts of Mrs Pengelley's visit to him. No one could have been more astonished than Dr Adams. His eyes almost started out of his head.

'God bless my soul!' he ejaculated. 'The poor woman must have been mad. Why didn't she speak to me? That was the proper thing to do.'

'And have her fears ridiculed?'

'Not at all, not at all. I hope I've got an open mind.'

Poirot looked at him and smiled. The physician was evidently more perturbed than he cared to admit. As we left the house, Poirot broke into a laugh.

'He is as obstinate as a pig, that one. He has said it is gastritis; therefore it is gastritis! All the same, he has the mind uneasy.'

'What's our next step?'

'A return to the inn, and a night of horror upon one of your English provincial beds, *mon ami*. It is a thing to make pity, the cheap English bed!'

'And tomorrow?'

'*Rien à faire*. We must return to town and await developments.'

'That's very tame,' I said, disappointed. 'Suppose there are none?'

'There will be! I can promise you that. Our old

doctor may give as many certificates as he pleases. He cannot stop several hundred tongues from wagging. And they will wag to some purpose, I can tell you that!'

Our train for town left at eleven the following morning. Before we started for the station, Poirot expressed a wish to see Miss Freda Stanton, the niece mentioned to us by the dead woman. We found the house where she was lodging easily enough. With her was a tall, dark young man whom she introduced in some confusion as Mr Jacob Radnor.

Miss Freda Stanton was an extremely pretty girl of the old Cornish type—dark hair and eyes and rosy cheeks. There was a flash in those same dark eyes which told of a temper that it would not be wise to provoke.

'Poor Auntie,' she said, when Poirot had introduced himself, and explained his business. 'It's terribly sad. I've been wishing all the morning that I'd been kinder and more patient.'

'You stood a great deal, Freda,' interrupted Radnor.

'Yes, Jacob, but I've got a sharp temper, I know. After all, it was only silliness on Auntie's part. I ought to have just laughed and not minded. Of course, it's all nonsense her thinking that Uncle was poisoning her. She *was* worse after any food he gave her—but I'm sure it was only from thinking about it. She made up her mind she would be, and then she was.'

'What was the actual cause of your disagreement, mademoiselle?'

Miss Stanton hesitated, looking at Radnor. That young gentleman was quick to take the hint.

'I must be getting along, Freda. See you this evening.

Goodbye, gentlemen; you're on your way to the station, I suppose?'

Poirot replied that we were, and Radnor departed.

'You are affianced, is it not so?' demanded Poirot, with a sly smile.

Freda Stanton blushed and admitted that such was the case.

'And that was really the whole trouble with Auntie,' she added.

'She did not approve of the match for you?'

'Oh, it wasn't that so much. But you see, she—' The girl came to a stop.

'Yes?' encouraged Poirot gently.

'It seems rather a horrid thing to say about her—now she's dead. But you'll never understand unless I tell you. Auntie was absolutely infatuated with Jacob.'

'Indeed?'

'Yes, wasn't it absurd? She was over fifty, and he's not quite thirty! But there it was. She was silly about him! I had to tell her at last that it was me he was after—and she carried on dreadfully. She wouldn't believe a word of it, and was so rude and insulting that it's no wonder I lost my temper. I talked it over with Jacob, and we agreed that the best thing to do was for me to clear out for a bit till she came to her senses. Poor Auntie—I suppose she was in a queer state altogether.'

'It would certainly seem so. Thank you, mademoiselle, for making things so clear to me.'

A little to my surprise, Radnor was waiting for us in the street below.

'I can guess pretty well what Freda has been telling

you,' he remarked. 'It was a most unfortunate thing to happen, and very awkward for me, as you can imagine. I need hardly say that it was none of my doing. I was pleased at first, because I imagined the old woman was helping on things with Freda. The whole thing was absurd—but extremely unpleasant.'

'When are you and Miss Stanton going to be married?'

'Soon, I hope. Now, M. Poirot, I'm going to be candid with you. I know a bit more than Freda does. She believes her uncle to be innocent. I'm not so sure. But I can tell you one thing: I'm going to keep my mouth shut about what I do know. Let sleeping dogs lie. I don't want my wife's uncle tried and hanged for murder.'

'Why do you tell me all this?'

'Because I've heard of you, and I know you're a clever man. It's quite possible that you might ferret out a case against him. But I put it to you—what good is that? The poor woman is past help, and she'd have been the last person to want a scandal—why, she'd turn in her grave at the mere thought of it.'

'You are probably right there. You want me to—hush it up, then?'

'That's my idea. I'll admit frankly that I'm selfish about it. I've got my way to make—and I'm building up a good little business as a tailor and outfitter.'

'Most of us are selfish, Mr Radnor. Not all of us admit it so freely. I will do what you ask—but I tell you frankly you will not succeed in hushing it up.'

'Why not?'

Poirot held up a finger. It was market day, and we were passing the market—a busy hum came from within.

'The voice of the people—that is why, Mr Radnor. Ah, we must run, or we shall miss our train.'

'Very interesting, is it not, Hastings?' said Poirot, as the train steamed out of the station.

He had taken out a small comb from his pocket, also a microscopic mirror, and was carefully arranging his moustache, the symmetry of which had become slightly impaired during our brisk run.

'You seem to find it so,' I replied. 'To me, it is all rather sordid and unpleasant. There's hardly any mystery about it.'

'I agree with you; there is no mystery whatever.'

'I suppose we can accept the girl's rather extraordinary story of her aunt's infatuation? That seemed the only fishy part to me. She was such a nice, respectable woman.'

'There is nothing extraordinary about that—it is completely ordinary. If you read the papers carefully, you will find that often a nice respectable woman of that age leaves a husband she has lived with for twenty years, and sometimes a whole family of children as well, in order to link her life with that of a young man considerably her junior. You admire *les femmes*, Hastings; you prostrate yourself before all of them who are good-looking and have the good taste to smile upon you; but psychologically you know nothing whatever about them. In the autumn of a woman's life, there comes always one mad moment when she longs for romance, for adventure—before it is too late. It comes none the less surely to a woman because she is the wife of a respectable dentist in a country town!'

'And you think—'

'That a clever man might take advantage of such a moment.'

'I shouldn't call Pengelley so clever,' I mused. 'He's got the whole town by the ears. And yet I suppose you're right. The only two men who know anything, Radnor and the doctor, both want to hush it up. He's managed that somehow. I wish we'd seen the fellow.'

'You can indulge your wish. Return by the next train and invent an aching molar.'

I looked at him keenly.

'I wish I knew what you considered so interesting about the case.'

'My interest is very aptly summed up by a remark of yours, Hastings. After interviewing the maid, you observed that for someone who was not going to say a word, she had said a good deal.'

'Oh!' I said doubtfully; then I harped back to my original criticism: 'I wonder why you made no attempt to see Pengelley?'

'*Mon ami*, I give him just three months. Then I shall see him for as long as I please—in the dock.'

For once I thought Poirot's prognostications were going to be proved wrong. The time went by, and nothing transpired as to our Cornish case. Other matters occupied us, and I had nearly forgotten the Pengelley tragedy when it was suddenly recalled to me by a short paragraph in the paper which stated that an order to exhume the body of Mrs Pengelley had been obtained from the Home Secretary.

A few days later, and 'The Cornish Mystery' was the

topic of every paper. It seemed that gossip had never entirely died down, and when the engagement of the widower to Miss Marks, his secretary, was announced, the tongues burst out again louder than ever. Finally a petition was sent to the Home Secretary; the body was exhumed; large quantities of arsenic were discovered; and Mr Pengelley was arrested and charged with the murder of his wife.

Poirot and I attended the preliminary proceedings. The evidence was much as might have been expected. Dr Adams admitted that the symptoms of arsenical poisoning might easily be mistaken for those of gastritis. The Home Office expert gave his evidence; the maid Jessie poured out a flood of voluble information, most of which was rejected, but which certainly strengthened the case against the prisoner. Freda Stanton gave evidence as to her aunt's being worse whenever she ate food prepared by her husband. Jacob Radnor told how he had dropped in unexpectedly on the day of Mrs Pengelley's death, and found Pengelley replacing the bottle of weed-killer on the pantry shelf, Mrs Pengelley's gruel being on the table close by. Then Miss Marks, the fair-haired secretary, was called, and wept and went into hysterics and admitted that there had been 'passages' between her and her employer, and that he had promised to marry her in the event of anything happening to his wife. Pengelley reserved his defence and was sent for trial.

Jacob Radnor walked back with us to our lodgings.

'You see, Mr Radnor,' said Poirot, 'I was right. The voice of the people spoke—and with no uncertain voice. There was to be no hushing up of this case.'

'You were quite right,' sighed Radnor. 'Do you see any chance of his getting off?'

'Well, he has reserved his defence. He may have something—up the sleeve, as you English say. Come in with us, will you not?'

Radnor accepted the invitation. I ordered two whiskies and sodas and a cup of chocolate. The last order caused consternation, and I much doubted whether it would ever put in an appearance.

'Of course,' continued Poirot, 'I have a good deal of experience in matters of this kind. And I see only one loophole of escape for our friend.'

'What is it?'

'That you should sign this paper.'

With the suddenness of a conjuror, he produced a sheet of paper covered with writing.

'What is it?'

'A confession that *you* murdered Mrs Pengelley.'

There was a moment's pause; then Radnor laughed.

'You must be mad!'

'No, no, my friend, I am not mad. You came here; you started a little business; you were short of money. Mr Pengelley was a man very well-to-do. You met his niece; she was inclined to smile upon you. But the small allowance that Pengelley might have given her upon her marriage was not enough for you. You must get rid of both the uncle and the aunt; then the money would come to her, since she was the only relative. How cleverly you set about it! You made love to that plain middle-aged woman until she was your slave. You implanted in her doubts of her husband. She discovered first that he was deceiving her—then, under your guidance, that

127

he was trying to poison her. You were often at the house; you had opportunities to introduce the arsenic into her food. But you were careful never to do so when her husband was away. Being a woman, she did not keep her suspicions to herself. She talked to her niece; doubtless she talked to other women friends. Your only difficulty was keeping up separate relations with the two women, and even that was not so difficult as it looked. You explained to the aunt that, to allay the suspicions of her husband, you had to pretend to pay court to the niece. And the younger lady needed little convincing—she would never seriously consider her aunt as a rival.

'But then Mrs Pengelley made up her mind, without saying anything to you, to consult *me*. If she could be really assured, beyond any possible doubt, that her husband was trying to poison her, she would feel justified in leaving him, and linking her life with yours—which is what she imagined you wanted her to do. But that did not suit your book at all. You did not want a detective prying around. A favourable minute occurs. You are in the house when Mr Pengelley is getting some gruel for his wife, and you introduce the fatal dose. The rest is easy. Apparently anxious to hush matters up, you secretly foment them. But you reckoned without Hercule Poirot, my intelligent young friend.'

Radnor was deadly pale, but he still endeavoured to carry off matters with a high hand.

'Very interesting and ingenious, but why tell me all this?'

'Because, monsieur, I represent—not the law, but Mrs Pengelley. For her sake, I give you a chance of escape. Sign this paper, and you shall have twenty-four hours' start—twenty-four hours before I place it in the hands of the police.'

Radnor hesitated.

'You can't prove anything.'

'Can't I? I am Hercule Poirot. Look out of the window, monsieur. There are two men in the street. They have orders not to lose sight of you.'

Radnor strode across to the window and pulled aside the blind, then shrank back with an oath.

'You see, monsieur? Sign—it is your best chance.'

'What guarantee have I—'

'That I shall keep faith? The word of Hercule Poirot. You will sign? Good. Hastings, be so kind as to pull that left-hand blind half-way up. That is the signal that Mr Radnor may leave unmolested.'

White, muttering oaths, Radnor hurried from the room. Poirot nodded gently.

'A coward! I always knew it.'

'It seems to me, Poirot, that you've acted in a criminal manner,' I cried angrily. 'You always preach against sentiment. And here you are letting a dangerous criminal escape out of sheer sentimentality.'

'That was not sentiment—that was business,' replied Poirot. 'Do you not see, my friend, that we have no shadow of proof against him? Shall I get up and say to twelve stolid Cornishmen that *I*, Hercule Poirot, *know*? They would laugh at me. The only chance was to frighten him and get a confession that way. Those two loafers that I noticed outside came in very useful. Pull down the blind again, will you, Hastings. Not that there was any reason for raising it. It was part of our *mise en scène*.

'Well, well, we must keep our word. Twenty-four hours, did I say? So much longer for poor Mr Pengelley—and it is not more than he deserves; for mark you, he deceived his wife. I am very strong on the family life, as you know. Ah, well, twenty-four hours—and then? I have great faith in Scotland Yard. They will get him, *mon ami*; they will get him.'

# The Regatta Mystery

Mr Isaac Pointz removed a cigar from his lips and said approvingly:

'Pretty little place.'

Having thus set the seal of his approval upon Dartmouth harbour, he replaced the cigar and looked about him with the air of a man pleased with himself, his appearance, his surroundings and life generally.

As regards the first of these, Mr Isaac Pointz was a man of fifty-eight, in good health and condition with perhaps a slight tendency to liver. He was not exactly stout, but comfortable-looking, and a yachting costume, which he wore at the moment, is not the most kindly of attires for a middle-aged man with a tendency to embonpoint. Mr Pointz was very well turned out—correct to every crease and button—his dark and slightly Oriental face beaming out under the peak of his yachting cap. As regards his surroundings, these may have been taken to mean his companions—his partner Mr Leo Stein, Sir George and Lady Marroway, an American business acquaintance Mr Samuel Leathern and his schoolgirl daughter Eve, Mrs Rustington and Evan Llewellyn.

The party had just come ashore from Mr Pointz' yacht—the *Merrimaid*. In the morning they had watched the yacht racing and they had now come ashore to join for a while in the fun of the fair—Coconut shies, Fat Ladies, the Human Spider and the Merry-go-round. It is hardly to be doubted that these delights were relished most by Eve Leathern. When Mr Pointz finally suggested that it was time to adjourn to the Royal George for dinner hers was the only dissentient voice.

'Oh, Mr Pointz—I did so want to have my fortune told by the Real Gypsy in the Caravan.'

Mr Pointz had doubts of the essential Realness of the Gypsy in question but he gave indulgent assent.

'Eve's just crazy about the fair,' said her father apologetically. 'But don't you pay any attention if you want to be getting along.'

'Plenty of time,' said Mr Pointz benignantly. 'Let the little lady enjoy herself. I'll take you on at darts, Leo.'

'Twenty-five and over wins a prize,' chanted the man in charge of the darts in a high nasal voice.

'Bet you a fiver my total score beats yours,' said Pointz.

'Done,' said Stein with alacrity.

The two men were soon whole-heartedly engaged in their battle.

Lady Marroway murmured to Evan Llewellyn:

'Eve is not the only child in the party.'

Llewellyn smiled assent but somewhat absently.

He had been absent-minded all that day. Once or twice his answers had been wide of the point.

Pamela Marroway drew away from him and said to her husband:

'That young man has something on his mind.'

Sir George murmured:

'Or someone?'

And his glance swept quickly over Janet Rustington.

Lady Marroway frowned a little. She was a tall woman exquisitely groomed. The scarlet of her fingernails was matched by the dark red coral studs in her ears. Her eyes were dark and watchful. Sir George affected a careless 'hearty English gentleman' manner—but his bright blue eyes held the same watchful look as his wife's.

Isaac Pointz and Leo Stein were Hatton Garden diamond merchants. Sir George and Lady Marroway came from a different world—the world of Antibes and Juan les Pins—of golf at St Jean-de-Luz—of bathing from the rocks at Madeira in the winter.

In outward seeming they were as the lilies that toiled not, neither did they spin. But perhaps this was not quite true. There are diverse ways of toiling and also of spinning.

'Here's the kid back again,' said Evan Llewellyn to Mrs Rustington.

He was a dark young man—there was a faintly hungry wolfish look about him which some women found attractive.

It was difficult to say whether Mrs Rustington found him so. She did not wear her heart on her sleeve. She had married young—and the marriage had ended in disaster in less than a year. Since that time it was difficult to know what Janet Rustington thought of anyone or anything—her manner was always the same—charming but completely aloof.

Eve Leathern came dancing up to them, her lank fair

hair bobbing excitedly. She was fifteen—an awkward child—but full of vitality.

'I'm going to be married by the time I'm seventeen,' she exclaimed breathlessly. 'To a very rich man and we're going to have six children and Tuesdays and Thursdays are my lucky days and I ought always to wear green or blue and an emerald is my lucky stone and—'

'Why, pet, I think we ought to be getting along,' said her father.

Mr Leathern was a tall, fair, dyspeptic-looking man with a somewhat mournful expression.

Mr Pointz and Mr Stein were turning away from the darts. Mr Pointz was chuckling and Mr Stein was looking somewhat rueful.

'It's all a matter of luck,' he was saying.

Mr Pointz slapped his pocket cheerfully.

'Took a fiver off you all right. Skill, my boy, skill. My old Dad was a first class darts player. Well, folks, let's be getting along. Had your fortune told, Eve? Did they tell you to beware of a dark man?'

'A dark woman,' corrected Eve. 'She's got a cast in her eye and she'll be real mean to me if I give her a chance. And I'm to be married by the time I'm seventeen . . .'

She ran on happily as the party steered its way to the Royal George.

Dinner had been ordered beforehand by the forethought of Mr Pointz and a bowing waiter led them upstairs and into a private room on the first floor. Here a round table was ready laid. The big bulging bow-window opened on the harbour square and was open. The noise of the fair came up to them, and the raucous squeal of three roundabouts each blaring a different tune.

'Best shut that if we're to hear ourselves speak,' observed Mr Pointz drily, and suited the action to the word.

They took their seats round the table and Mr Pointz beamed affectionately at his guests. He felt he was doing them well and he liked to do people well. His eye rested on one after another. Lady Marroway—fine woman—not quite the goods, of course, he knew that—he was perfectly well aware that what he had called all his life the *crème de la crème* would have very little to do with the Marroways—but then the *crème de la crème* were supremely unaware of his own existence. Anyway, Lady Marroway was a damned smart-looking woman—and he didn't mind if she *did* rook him at Bridge. Didn't enjoy it quite so much from Sir George. Fishy eye the fellow had. Brazenly on the make. But he wouldn't make too much out of Isaac Pointz. He'd see to that all right.

Old Leathern wasn't a bad fellow—longwinded, of course, like most Americans—fond of telling endless long stories. And he had that disconcerting habit of requiring precise information. What was the population of Dartmouth? In what year had the Naval College been built? And so on. Expected his host to be a kind of walking Baedeker. Eve was a nice cheery kid—he enjoyed chaffing her. Voice rather like a corncrake, but she had all her wits about her. A bright kid.

Young Llewellyn—he seemed a bit quiet. Looked as though he had something on his mind. Hard up, probably. These writing fellows usually were. Looked as though he might be keen on Janet Rustington. A nice woman—attractive and clever, too. But she didn't ram her writing down your throat. Highbrow sort of stuff

135

she wrote but you'd never think it to hear her talk. And old Leo! *He* wasn't getting younger or thinner. And blissfully unaware that his partner was at that moment thinking precisely the same thing about him, Mr Pointz corrected Mr Leathern as to pilchards being connected with Devon and not Cornwall, and prepared to enjoy his dinner.

'Mr Pointz,' said Eve when plates of hot mackerel had been set before them and the waiters had left the room.

'Yes, young lady.'

'Have you got that big diamond with you right now? The one you showed us last night and said you always took about with you?'

Mr Pointz chuckled.

'That's right. My mascot, I call it. Yes, I've got it with me all right.'

'I think that's awfully dangerous. Somebody might get it away from you in the crowd at the fair.'

'Not they,' said Mr Pointz. 'I'll take good care of that.'

'But they *might*,' insisted Eve. 'You've got gangsters in England as well as we have, haven't you?'

'They won't get the Morning Star,' said Mr Pointz. 'To begin with it's in a special inner pocket. And anyway—old Pointz knows what he's about. Nobody's going to steal the Morning Star.'

Eve laughed.

'Ugh-huh—bet I could steal it!'

'I bet you couldn't.' Mr Pointz twinkled back at her.

'Well, I bet I could. I was thinking about it last night in bed—after you'd handed it round the table, for us all to look at. I thought of a real cute way to steal it.'

'And what's that?'

Eve put her head on one side, her fair hair wagged excitedly. 'I'm not telling you—now. What do you bet I couldn't?'

Memories of Mr Pointz's youth rose in his mind.

'Half a dozen pairs of gloves,' he said.

'Gloves,' cried Eve disgustedly. 'Who wears gloves?'

'Well—do you wear nylon stockings?'

'Do I not? My best pair ran this morning.'

'Very well, then. Half a dozen pairs of the finest nylon stockings—'

'Oo-er,' said Eve blissfully. 'And what about you?'

'Well, I need a new tobacco pouch.'

'Right. That's a deal. Not that you'll get your tobacco pouch. Now I'll tell you what you've got to do. You must hand it round like you did last night—'

She broke off as two waiters entered to remove the plates. When they were starting on the next course of chicken, Mr Pointz said:

'Remember this, young woman, if this is to represent a real theft, I should send for the police and you'd be searched.'

'That's quite OK by me. You needn't be quite so life-like as to bring the police into it. But Lady Marroway or Mrs Rustington can do all the searching you like.'

'Well, that's that then,' said Mr Pointz. 'What are you setting up to be? A first class jewel thief?'

'I might take to it as a career—if it really paid.'

'If you got away with the Morning Star it would pay you. Even after recutting that stone would be worth over thirty thousand pounds.'

'My!' said Eve, impressed. 'What's that in dollars?'

Lady Marroway uttered an exclamation.

'And you carry such a stone about with you?' she said reproachfully. 'Thirty thousand pounds.' Her darkened eyelashes quivered.

Mrs Rustington said softly: 'It's a lot of money . . . And then there's the fascination of the stone itself . . . It's beautiful.'

'Just a piece of carbon,' said Evan Llewellyn.

'I've always understood it's the "fence" that's the difficulty in jewel robberies,' said Sir George. 'He takes the lion's share—eh, what?'

'Come on,' said Eve excitedly. 'Let's start. Take the diamond out and say what you said last night.'

Mr Leathern said in his deep melancholy voice, 'I do apologize for my offspring. She gets kinder worked up—'

'That'll do, Pops,' said Eve. 'Now then, Mr Pointz—'

Smiling, Mr Pointz fumbled in an inner pocket. He drew something out. It lay on the palm of his hand, blinking in the light.

'A diamond . . .'

Rather stiffly, Mr Pointz repeated as far as he could remember his speech of the previous evening on the *Merrimaid*.

'Perhaps you ladies and gentlemen would like to have a look at this? It's an unusually beautiful stone. I call it the Morning Star and it's by way of being my mascot—goes about with me anywhere. Like to see it?'

He handed it to Lady Marroway, who took it, exclaimed at its beauty and passed it to Mr Leathern who said, 'Pretty good—yes, pretty good,' in a somewhat artificial manner and in his turn passed it to Llewellyn.

The waiters coming in at that moment, there was a slight hitch in the proceedings. When they had gone again, Evan said, 'Very fine stone,' and passed it to Leo Stein who did not trouble to make any comment but handed it quickly on to Eve.

'How perfectly lovely,' cried Eve in a high affected voice.

'Oh!' She gave a cry of consternation as it slipped from her hand. 'I've dropped it.'

She pushed back her chair and got down to grope under the table. Sir George at her right, bent also. A glass got swept off the table in the confusion. Stein, Llewellyn and Mrs Rustington all helped in the search. Finally Lady Marroway joined in.

Only Mr Pointz took no part in the proceedings. He remained in his seat sipping his wine and smiling sardonically.

'Oh, dear,' said Eve, still in her artificial manner, 'How dreadful! Where *can* it have rolled to? I can't find it anywhere.'

One by one the assistant searchers rose to their feet. 'It's disappeared all right, Pointz,' said Sir George smiling.

'Very nicely done,' said Mr Pointz, nodding approval. 'You'd make a very good actress, Eve. Now the question is, have you hidden it somewhere or have you got it on you?'

'Search me,' said Eve dramatically.

Mr Pointz' eye sought out a large screen in the corner of the room.

He nodded towards it and then looked at Lady Marroway and Mrs Rustington.

'If you ladies will be so good—'

'Why, certainly,' said Lady Marroway, smiling.

The two women rose.

Lady Marroway said, 'Don't be afraid, Mr Pointz. We'll vet her properly.'

The three went behind the screen.

The room was hot. Evan Llewellyn flung open the window. A news vendor was passing. Evan threw down a coin and the man threw up a paper.

Llewellyn unfolded it.

'Hungarian situation's none too good,' he said.

'That the local rag?' asked Sir George. 'There's a horse I'm interested in ought to have run at Haldon today— Natty Boy.'

'Leo,' said Mr Pointz. 'Lock the door. We don't want those damned waiters popping in and out till this business is over.'

'Natty Boy won three to one,' said Evan.

'Rotten odds,' said Sir George.

'Mostly Regatta news,' said Evan, glancing over the sheet.

The three young women came out from the screen.

'Not a sign of it,' said Janet Rustington.

'You can take it from me she hasn't got it on her,' said Lady Marroway.

Mr Pointz thought he would be quite ready to take it from her. There was a grim tone in her voice and he felt no doubt that the search had been thorough.

'Say, Eve, you haven't swallowed it?' asked Mr Leathern anxiously. 'Because maybe that wouldn't be too good for you.'

'I'd have seen her do that,' said Leo Stein quietly. 'I was watching her. She didn't put anything in her mouth.'

'I couldn't swallow a great thing all points like that,' said Eve. She put her hands on her hips and looked at Mr Pointz. 'What about it, big boy?' she asked.

'You stand over there where you are and don't move,' said that gentleman.

Among them, the men stripped the table and turned it upside down. Mr Pointz examined every inch of it. Then he transferred his attention to the chair on which Eve had been sitting and those on either side of her.

The thoroughness of the search left nothing to be desired. The other four men joined in and the women also. Eve Leathern stood by the wall near the screen and laughed with intense enjoyment.

Five minutes later Mr Pointz rose with a slight groan from his knees and dusted his trousers sadly. His pristine freshness was somewhat impaired.

'Eve,' he said. 'I take off my hat to you. You're the finest thing in jewel thieves I've ever come across. What you've done with that stone beats me. As far as I can see it must be in the room as it isn't on you. I give you best.'

'Are the stockings mine?' demanded Eve.

'They're yours, young lady.'

'Eve, my child, where *can* you have hidden it?' demanded Mrs Rustington curiously.

Eve pranced forward.

'I'll show you. You'll all be just mad with yourselves.'

She went across to the side table where the things from the dinner table had been roughly stacked. She picked up her little black evening bag—

'Right under your eyes. Right . . .'

Her voice, gay and triumphant, trailed off suddenly.

'Oh,' she said. '*Oh . . .*'

'What's the matter, honey?' said her father.

Eve whispered: 'It's gone . . . it's *gone* . . .'

'What's all this?' asked Pointz, coming forward.

Eve turned to him impetuously.

'It was like this. This pochette of mine has a big paste stone in the middle of the clasp. It fell out last night and just when you were showing that diamond round I noticed that it was much the same size. And so I thought in the night what a good idea for a robbery it would be to wedge your diamond into the gap with a bit of plasticine. I felt sure nobody would ever spot it. That's what I did tonight. First I dropped it—then went down after it with the bag in my hand, stuck it into the gap with a bit of plasticine which I had handy, put my bag on the table and went on pretending to look for the diamond. I thought it would be like the Purloined Letter—you know—lying there in full view under all your noses—and just looking like a common bit of rhinestone. And it was a good plan—none of you *did* notice.'

'I wonder,' said Mr Stein.

'What did you say?'

Mr Pointz took the bag, looked at the empty hole with a fragment of plasticine still adhering to it and said slowly: 'It may have fallen out. We'd better look again.'

The search was repeated, but this time it was a curiously silent business. An atmosphere of tension pervaded the room.

Finally everyone in turn gave it up. They stood looking at each other.

'It's not in this room,' said Stein.

'And nobody's left the room,' said Sir George significantly.

There was a moment's pause. Eve burst into tears.

Her father patted her on the shoulder.

'There, there,' he said awkwardly.

Sir George turned to Leo Stein.

'Mr Stein,' he said. 'Just now you murmured something under your breath. When I asked you to repeat it, you said it was nothing. But as a matter of fact I heard what you said. Miss Eve had just said that none of us noticed the place where she had put the diamond. The words you murmured were: "I wonder." What we have to face is the probability that one person *did* notice—that that person is in this room now. I suggest that the only fair and honourable thing is for every one present to submit to a search. The diamond cannot have left the room.'

When Sir George played the part of the old English gentleman, none could play it better. His voice rang with sincerity and indignation.

'Bit unpleasant, all this,' said Mr Pointz unhappily.

'It's all my fault,' sobbed Eve. 'I didn't mean—'

'Buck up, kiddo,' said Mr Stein kindly. 'Nobody's blaming you.'

Mr Leathern said in his slow pedantic manner:

'Why, certainly, I think that Sir George's suggestion will meet with the fullest approval from all of us. It does from me.'

'I agree,' said Evan Llewellyn.

Mrs Rustington looked at Lady Marroway who nodded a brief assent. The two of them went back behind the screen and the sobbing Eve accompanied them.

A waiter knocked on the door and was told to go away.

Five minutes later eight people looked at each other incredulously.

The Morning Star had vanished into space . . .

Mr Parker Pyne looked thoughtfully at the dark agitated face of the young man opposite him.

'Of course,' he said. 'You're Welsh, Mr Llewellyn.'

'What's that got to do with it?'

Mr Parker Pyne waved a large, well-cared-for hand.

'Nothing at all, I admit. I am interested in the classification of emotional reactions as exemplified by certain racial types. That is all. Let us return to the consideration of your particular problem.'

'I don't really know why I came to you,' said Evan Llewellyn. His hands twitched nervously, and his dark face had a haggard look. He did not look at Mr Parker Pyne and that gentleman's scrutiny seemed to make him uncomfortable. 'I don't know why I came to you,' he repeated. 'But where the Hell *can* I go? And what the Hell can I *do*? It's the powerlessness of not being able to do anything at all that gets me . . . I saw your advertisement and I remembered that a chap had once spoken of you and said that you got results . . . And—well—I came! I suppose I was a fool. It's the sort of position nobody can do anything about.'

'Not at all,' said Mr Parker Pyne. 'I am the proper person to come to. I am a specialist in unhappiness. This business has obviously caused you a good deal of pain. You are sure the facts are exactly as you have told me?'

'I don't think I've left out anything. Pointz brought out the diamond and passed it around—that wretched American child stuck it on her ridiculous bag and when

144

we came to look at the bag, the diamond was gone. It wasn't on anyone—old Pointz himself even was searched—he suggested it himself—and I'll swear it was nowhere in that room! *And nobody left the room*—'

'No waiters, for instance?' suggested Mr Parker Pyne.

Llewellyn shook his head.

'They went out before the girl began messing about with the diamond, and afterwards Pointz locked the door so as to keep them out. No, it lies between one of us.'

'It would certainly seem so,' said Mr Parker Pyne thoughtfully.

'That damned evening paper,' said Evan Llewellyn bitterly. 'I saw it come into their minds—that that was the only way—'

'Just tell me again exactly what occurred.'

'It was perfectly simple. I threw open the window, whistled to the man, threw down a copper and he tossed me up the paper. And there it is, you see—the only possible way the diamond could have left the room—thrown by me to an accomplice waiting in the street below.'

'Not the *only* possible way,' said Mr Parker Pyne.

'What other way can you suggest?'

'If you didn't throw it out, there *must* have been some other way.'

'Oh, I see. I hoped you meant something more definite than that. Well, I can only say that I *didn't* throw it out. I can't expect you to believe me—or anyone else.'

'Oh, yes, I believe you,' said Mr Parker Pyne.

'You do? Why?'

'Not a criminal type,' said Mr Parker Pyne. 'Not, that is, the particular criminal type that steals jewellery.

There are crimes, of course, that you might commit—but we won't enter into that subject. At any rate I do not see you as the purloiner of the Morning Star.'

'Everyone else does though,' said Llewellyn bitterly.

'I see,' said Mr Parker Pyne.

'They looked at me in a queer sort of way at the time. Marroway picked up the paper and just glanced over at the window. He didn't say anything. But Pointz cottoned on to it quick enough! I could see what they thought. There hasn't been any open accusation, that's the devil of it.'

Mr Parker Pyne nodded sympathetically.

'It is worse than that,' he said.

'Yes. It's just suspicion. I've had a fellow round asking questions—routine inquiries, he called it. One of the new dress-shirted lot of police, I suppose. Very tactful—nothing at all hinted. Just interested in the fact that I'd been hard up and was suddenly cutting a bit of a splash.'

'And were you?'

'Yes—some luck with a horse or two. Unluckily my bets were made on the course—there's nothing to show that that's how the money came in. They can't disprove it, of course—but that's just the sort of easy lie a fellow would invent if he didn't want to show where the money came from.'

'I agree. Still they will have to have a good deal more than that to go upon.'

'Oh! I'm not afraid of actually being arrested and charged with the theft. In a way that would be easier—one would know, where one was. It's the ghastly fact that all those people believe I took it.'

'One person in particular?'

'What do you mean?'

'A suggestion—nothing more—' Again Mr Parker Pyne waved his comfortable-looking hand. 'There *was* one person in particular, wasn't there? Shall we say Mrs Rustington?'

Llewellyn's dark face flushed.

'Why pitch on her?'

'Oh, my dear sir—there is obviously someone whose opinion matters to you greatly—probably a lady. What ladies were there? An American flapper? Lady Marroway? But you would probably rise not fall in Lady Marroway's estimation if you had brought off such a coup. I know something of the lady. Clearly then, Mrs Rustington.'

Llewellyn said with something of an effort,

'She—she's had rather an unfortunate experience. Her husband was a down and out rotter. It's made her unwilling to trust anyone. She—if she thinks—'

He found it difficult to go on.

'Quite so,' said Mr Parker Pyne. 'I see the matter is important. It must be cleared up.'

Evan gave a short laugh.

'That's easy to say.'

'And quite easy to do,' said Mr Parker Pyne.

'You think so?'

'Oh, yes—the problem is so clear cut. So many possibilities are ruled out. `The answer must really be extremely simple. Indeed already I have a kind of glimmering—'

Llewellyn stared at him incredulously.

Mr Parker Pyne drew a pad of paper towards him and picked up a pen.

'Perhaps you would give me a brief description of the party.'

'Haven't I already done so?'

'Their personal appearance—colour of hair and so on.'

'But, Mr Parker Pyne, what can that have to do with it?'

'A good deal, young man, a good deal. Classification and so on.'

Somewhat unbelievingly, Evan described the personal appearance of the members of the yachting party.

Mr Parker Pyne made a note or two, pushed away the pad and said:

'Excellent. By the way, did you say a wine glass was broken?'

Evan stared again.

'Yes, it was knocked off the table and then it got stepped on.'

'Nasty thing, splinters of glass,' said Mr Parker Pyne. 'Whose wine glass was it?'

'I think it was the child's—Eve.'

'Ah!—and who sat next to her on that side?'

'Sir George Marroway.'

'You didn't see which of them knocked it off the table?'

'Afraid I didn't. Does it matter?'

'Not really. No. That was a superfluous question. Well'—he stood up—'good morning, Mr Llewellyn. Will you call again in three days' time? I think the whole thing will be quite satisfactorily cleared up by then.'

'Are you joking, Mr Parker Pyne?'

'I never joke on professional matters, my dear sir. It would occasion distrust in my clients. Shall we say Friday at eleven-thirty? Thank you.'

Evan entered Mr Parker Pyne's office on the Friday morning in a considerable turmoil. Hope and scepticism fought for mastery.

Mr Parker Pyne rose to meet him with a beaming smile.

'Good morning, Mr Llewellyn. Sit down. Have a cigarette?'

Llewellyn waved aside the proffered box.

'Well?' he said.

'Very well indeed,' said Mr Parker Pyne. 'The police arrested the gang last night.'

'The gang? What gang?'

'The Amalfi gang. I thought of them at once when you told me your story. I recognized their methods and once you had described the guests, well, there was no doubt at all in my mind.'

'Who are the Amalfi gang?'

'Father, son and daughter-in-law—that is if Pietro and Maria are really married—which some doubt.'

'I don't understand.'

'It's quite simple. The name is Italian and no doubt the origin is Italian, but old Amalfi was born in America. His methods are usually the same. He impersonates a real business man, introduces himself to some prominent figure in the jewel business in some European country and then plays his little trick. In this case he was deliberately on the track of the Morning Star. Pointz' idiosyncrasy was well known in the trade. Maria Amalfi played the part of his daughter (amazing creature, twenty-seven at least, and nearly always plays a part of sixteen).'

'Not Eve!' gasped Llewellyn.

'Exactly. The third member of the gang got himself taken on as an extra waiter at the Royal George—it was holiday time, remember, and they would need extra staff. He may even have bribed a regular man to stay away. The scene is set. Eve challenges old Pointz and he takes on the bet. He passes round the diamond as he had done the night before. The waiters enter the room and Leathern retains the stone until they have left the room. When they do leave, the diamond leaves also, neatly attached with a morsel of chewing gum to the underside of the plate that Pietro bears away. So simple!'

'But I *saw* it after that.'

'No, no, you saw a paste replica, good enough to deceive a casual glance. Stein, you told me, hardly looked at it. Eve drops it, sweeps off a glass too and steps firmly on stone and glass together. Miraculous disappearance of diamond. Both Eve and Leathern can submit to as much searching as anyone pleases.'

'Well—I'm—' Evan shook his head, at a loss for words.

'You say you recognized the gang from my description. Had they worked this trick before?'

'Not exactly—but it was their kind of business. Naturally my attention was at once directed to the girl Eve.'

'Why? I didn't suspect her—nobody did. She seemed such a—such a *child*.'

'That is the peculiar genius of Maria Amalfi. She is more like a child than any child could possibly be! And then the plasticine! This bet was supposed to have arisen quite spontaneously—yet the little lady had some plasticine with her all handy. That spoke of premeditation. My suspicions fastened on her at once.'

Llewellyn rose to his feet.

'Well, Mr Parker Pyne, I'm no end obliged to you.'

'Classification,' murmured Mr Parker Pyne. 'The classification of criminal types—it interests me.'

'You'll let me know how much—er—'

'My fee will be quite moderate,' said Mr Parker Pyne. 'It will not make too big a hole in the—er—horse racing profits. All the same, young man, I should, I think, leave the horses alone in future. Very uncertain animal, the horse.'

'That's all right,' said Evan.

He shook Mr Parker Pyne by the hand and strode from the office.

He hailed a taxi and gave the address of Janet Rustington's flat.

He felt in a mood to carry all before him.

# The Flock of Geryon

'I really do apologize for intruding like this, M. Poirot.'

Miss Carnaby clasped her hands fervently round her handbag and leaned forward, peering anxiously into Poirot's face. As usual, she sounded breathless.

Hercule Poirot's eyebrows rose.

She said anxiously:

'You do remember me, don't you?'

Hercule Poirot's eyes twinkled. He said:

'I remember you as one of the most successful criminals I have ever encountered!'

'Oh dear me, M. Poirot, must you really say such things? You *were* so kind to me. Emily and I often talk about you, and if we see anything about you in the paper we cut it out at once and paste it in a book. As for Augustus, we have taught him a new trick. We say, "Die for Sherlock Holmes, die for Mr Fortune, die for Sir Henry Merrivale, and then *die for M. Hercule Poirot*" and he goes down and lies like a *log*—lies absolutely still without moving until we say the word!'

'I am gratified,' said Poirot. 'And how is *ce cher Auguste*?'

152

Miss Carnaby clasped her hands and became eloquent in praise of her Pekinese.

'Oh, M. Poirot, he's cleverer than ever. He knows *everything*. Do you know, the other day I was just admiring a baby in a pram and suddenly I felt a tug and there was Augustus trying his hardest to bite through his lead. Wasn't that clever?'

Poirot's eyes twinkled. He said:

'It looks to me as though Augustus shared these criminal tendencies we were speaking of just now!'

Miss Carnaby did not laugh. Instead, her nice plump face grew worried and sad. She said in a kind of gasp:

'Oh, M. Poirot, I'm so *worried.*'

Poirot said kindly:

'What is it?'

'Do you know, M. Poirot, I'm afraid—I really am afraid—that I must be a *hardened criminal*—if I may use such a term. Ideas come to me!'

'What kind of ideas?'

'The most extraordinary ideas! For instance, yesterday, a really most *practical* scheme for robbing a post office came into my head. I wasn't thinking about it—it just came! And another very ingenious way for evading custom duties... I feel convinced—quite convinced—that it would work.'

'It probably would,' said Poirot drily. 'That is the danger of your ideas.'

'It has worried me, M. Poirot, very much. Having been brought up with strict principles, as I have been, it is *most* disturbing that such lawless—such really *wicked*—ideas should come to me. The trouble is partly, I think, that I have a good deal of leisure time now. I have left

Lady Hoggin and I am engaged by an old lady to read to her and write her letters every day. The letters are soon done and the moment I begin reading she goes to sleep, so I am left just sitting there—with an idle mind—and we all know the use the devil has for idleness.'

'Tcha, tcha,' said Poirot.

'Recently I have read a book—a very modern book, translated from the German. It throws a most interesting light on criminal tendencies. One must, so I understand, *sublimate* one's impulses! That, really, is why I came to you.'

'Yes?' said Poirot.

'You see, M. Poirot. I think that it is really not so much *wickedness* as a craving for excitement! My life has unfortunately been very humdrum. The—er—campaign of the Pekinese dogs, I sometimes feel, was the only time I really *lived*. Very reprehensible, of course, but, as my book says, one must not turn one's back on the truth. I came to you, M. Poirot, because I hoped it might be possible to—to sublimate that craving for excitement by employing it, if I may put it that way, on the side of the angels.'

'Aha,' said Poirot. 'It is then as a colleague that you present yourself?'

Miss Carnaby blushed.

'It is very presumptuous of me, I know. But you were so *kind*—'

She stopped. Her eyes, faded blue eyes, had something in them of the pleading of a dog who hopes against hope that you will take him for a walk.

'It is an idea,' said Hercule Poirot slowly.

'I am, of course, not at all clever,' explained Miss

Carnaby. 'But my powers of—of dissimulation are good. They have to be—otherwise one would be discharged from the post of companion immediately. And I have always found that to appear even stupider than one is, occasionally has good results.'

Hercule Poirot laughed. He said:

'You enchant me, Mademoiselle.'

'Oh dear, M. Poirot, what a very kind man you are. Then you do encourage me to *hope*? As it happens, I have just received a small legacy—a very small one, but it enables my sister and myself to keep and feed ourselves in a frugal manner so that I am not absolutely dependent on what I earn.'

'I must consider,' said Poirot, 'where your talents may best be employed. You have no idea yourself, I suppose?'

'You know, you must really be a thought reader, M. Poirot. I *have* been anxious lately about a friend of mine. I was going to consult you. Of course you may say it is all an old maid's fancy—just imagination. One is prone, perhaps, to exaggerate, and to see *design* where there may be only *coincidence*.'

'I do not think you would exaggerate, Miss Carnaby. Tell me what is on your mind.'

'Well, I have a friend, a very dear friend, though I have not seen very much of her of late years. Her name is Emmeline Clegg. She married a man in the North of England and he died a few years ago leaving her very comfortably off. She was unhappy and lonely after his death and I am afraid she is in some ways a rather foolish and perhaps credulous woman. Religion, M. Poirot, can be a great help and sustenance—but by that I mean orthodox religion.'

'You refer to the Greek Church?' asked Poirot.

Miss Carnaby looked shocked.

'Oh no, indeed. Church of England. And though I do not *approve* of Roman Catholics, they are at least *recognized*. And the Wesleyans and Congregationalists—they are all well-known respectable bodies. What I am talking about are these *odd* sects. They just spring up. They have a kind of emotional appeal but sometimes I have very grave doubts as to whether there is any true religious feeling behind them at all.'

'You think your friend is being victimized by a sect of this kind?'

'I do. Oh! I certainly do. The Flock of the Shepherd, they call themselves. Their headquarters is in Devonshire—a very lovely estate by the sea. The adherents go there for what they term a Retreat. That is a period of a fortnight—with religious services and rituals. And there are three big Festivals in the year, the Coming of the Pasture, the Full Pasture, and the Reaping of the Pasture.'

'Which last is stupid,' said Poirot. 'Because one does not reap pasture.'

'The whole thing is stupid,' said Miss Carnaby with warmth. 'The whole sect centres round the head of the movement, the Great Shepherd, he is called. A Dr Andersen. A very handsome-looking man, I believe, with a presence.'

'Which is attractive to the women, yes?'

'I am afraid so,' Miss Carnaby sighed. 'My father was a very handsome man. Sometimes, it was most awkward in the parish. The rivalry in embroidering vestments—and the division of church work...'

She shook her head reminiscently.

'Are the members of the Great Flock mostly women?'

'At least three quarters of them, I gather. What men there are, are mostly *cranks*! It is upon the women that the success of the movement depends and—and on the *funds* they supply.'

'Ah,' said Poirot. 'Now we come to it. Frankly, you think the whole thing is a ramp?'

'Frankly, M. Poirot, I do. And another thing worries me. I happen to know that my poor friend is so bound up in this religion that she has recently made a will leaving all her property to the movement.'

Poirot said sharply:

'Was that—suggested to her?'

'In all fairness, no. It was entirely her own idea. The Great Shepherd had shown her a new way of life—so all that she had was to go on her death to the Great Cause. What really worries me is—'

'Yes—go on—'

'Several wealthy women have been among the devotees. In the last year *three* of them, no less, have died.'

'Leaving all their money to this sect?'

'Yes.'

'Their relations have made no protest? I should have thought it likely that there might have been litigation.'

'You see, M. Poirot, it is usually *lonely* women who belong to this gathering. People who have no very near relations or friends.'

Poirot nodded thoughtfully. Miss Carnaby hurried on:

'Of course I've no right to suggest anything at all. From what I have been able to find out, there was nothing *wrong* about any of these deaths. One, I believe, was *pneumonia* following *influenza* and another was attributed to gastric ulcer. There were absolutely no *suspicious circumstances*, if you know what I mean, and the deaths did not take place at Green Hills Sanctuary, but at their own homes. I've no doubt it is *quite* all right, but all the same I—well—I shouldn't like anything to happen to Emmie.'

She clasped her hands, her eyes appealed to Poirot.

Poirot himself was silent for some minutes. When he spoke there was a change in his voice. It was grave and deep.

He said:

'Will you give me, or will you find out for me, the names and addresses of these members of the sect who have recently died?'

'Yes indeed, M. Poirot.'

Poirot said slowly:

'Mademoiselle, I think you are a woman of great courage and determination. You have good histrionic powers. Would you be willing to undertake a piece of work that may be attended with considerable danger?'

'I should like nothing better,' said the adventurous Miss Carnaby.

Poirot said warningly:

'If there is a risk at all, it will be a grave one. You comprehend—either this is a mare's nest or it is *serious*. To find out which it is, it will be necessary for you yourself to become a member of the Great Flock. I would suggest that you exaggerate the amount of the legacy that you recently inherited. You are now a well-to-do woman with no very definite aim in life. You argue with your friend Emmeline about this religion she has

158

adopted—assure her that it is all nonsense. She is eager to convert you. You allow yourself to be persuaded to go down to Green Hills Sanctuary. And there you fall a victim to the persuasive powers and magnetic influence of Dr Andersen. I think I can safely leave that part to you?'

Miss Carnaby smiled modestly. She murmured:

'I think I can manage *that* all right!'

'Well, my friend, what have you got for me?'

Chief Inspector Japp looked thoughtfully at the little man who asked the question. He said ruefully:

'Not at all what I'd like to have, Poirot. I hate these long-haired, religious cranks like poison. Filling up women with a lot of mumbo-jumbo. But this fellow's being careful. There's nothing one can get hold of. All sounds a bit batty but harmless.'

'Have you learned anything about this Dr Andersen?'

'I've looked up his past history. He was a promising chemist and got chucked out of some German University. Seems his mother was Jewish. He was always keen on the study of Oriental Myths and Religions, spent all his spare time on that and has written various articles on the subject—some of the articles sound pretty crazy to me.'

'So it is possible that he is a genuine fanatic?'

'I'm bound to say it seems quite likely!'

'What about those names and addresses I gave you?'

'Nothing doing there. Miss Everitt died of ulcerative colitis. Doctor quite positive there was no hankypanky. Mrs Lloyd died of broncho-pneumonia. Lady Western died of tuberculosis. Had suffered from it many years ago—before she even met this bunch. Miss Lee died of typhoid—attributed to some salad she ate somewhere in the north of England. Three of them got ill and died in their own homes, and Mrs Lloyd died in a hotel in the south of France. As far as those deaths go, there's nothing to connect them with the Great Flock or with Andersen's place down in Devonshire. Must be pure coincidence. All absolutely O.K. and according to Cocker.'

Hercule Poirot sighed. He said:

'And yet, *mon cher*, I have a feeling that this is the tenth Labour of Hercules, and that this Dr Andersen is the Monster Geryon whom it is my mission to destroy.'

Japp looked at him anxiously.

'Look here, Poirot, you haven't been reading any queer literature yourself lately, have you?'

Poirot said with dignity:

'My remarks are, as always, apt, sound, and to the point.'

'You might start a new religion yourself,' said Japp, 'with the creed: "There is no one so clever as Hercule Poirot,

Amen, D.C. Repeat *ad lib*."!'

'It is the peace here that I find so wonderful,' said Miss Carnaby, breathing heavily and ecstatically.

'I told you so, Amy,' said Emmeline Clegg.

The two friends were sitting on the slope of a hillside overlooking a deep and lovely blue sea. The grass was vivid green, the earth and the cliffs a deep, glowing red. The little estate now known as Green Hills Sanctuary was a promontory comprising about six acres. Only a narrow neck of land joined it to the mainland so that it was almost an island.

Mrs Clegg murmured sentimentally:

'The red land—the land of glow and promise—where threefold destiny is to be accomplished.'

Miss Carnaby sighed deeply and said:

'I thought the Master put it all so beautifully at the service last night.'

'Wait,' said her friend, 'for the festival tonight. The Full Growth of the Pasture!'

'I'm looking forward to it,' said Miss Carnaby.

'You will find it a wonderful spiritual experience,' her friend promised her.

Miss Carnaby had arrived at Green Hills Sanctuary a week previously. Her attitude on arrival had been: 'Now what's all this nonsense? Really, Emmie, a sensible woman like you—etc., etc.'

At a preliminary interview with Dr Andersen, she had conscientiously made her position quite clear.

'I don't want to feel that I am here under false pretences, Dr Andersen. My father was a clergyman of the Church of England and I have never wavered in my faith. I don't hold with heathen doctrines.'

The big, golden-haired man had smiled at her—a very sweet and understanding smile. He had looked indulgently at the plump, rather belligerent figure sitting so squarely in her chair.

'Dear Miss Carnaby,' he said. 'You are Mrs Clegg's friend, and as such welcome. And believe me, our doctrines are not heathen. Here all religions are welcomed, and all honoured equally.'

'Then they shouldn't be,' said the staunch daughter of the late Reverend Thomas Carnaby.

Leaning back in his chair, the Master murmured in

his rich voice: 'In my Father's House are many mansions... Remember that, Miss Carnaby.'

As they left the presence, Miss Carnaby murmured to her friend: 'He really is a very handsome man.'

'Yes,' said Emmeline Clegg. 'And so wonderfully spiritual.'

Miss Carnaby agreed. It was true—she had felt it—an aura of unworldliness—of spirituality...

She took a grip upon herself. She was not here to fall a prey to the fascination, spiritual or otherwise, of the Great Shepherd. She conjured up a vision of Hercule Poirot. He seemed very far away, and curiously mundane...

'Amy,' said Miss Carnaby to herself. 'Take a grip upon yourself. Remember what you are here for...'

But as the days went on, she found herself surrendering only too easily to the spell of Green Hills. The peace, the simplicity, the delicious though simple food, the beauty of the services with their chants of Love and Worship, the simple moving words of the Master, appealing to all that was best and highest in humanity— here all the strife and ugliness of the world was shut out. Here was only Peace and Love...

And tonight was the great summer Festival, the Festival of the Full Pasture. And at it, she, Amy Carnaby, was to become initiated—to become one of the Flock.

The Festival took place in the white, glittering, concrete building, called by the Initiates the Sacred Fold. Here the devotees assembled just before the setting of the sun. They wore sheepskin cloaks and had sandals on their feet. Their arms were bare. In the centre of the Fold on a raised platform stood Dr Andersen. The big man, golden-haired and blue-eyed, with his fair beard and his handsome profile had never seemed more compelling. He was dressed in a green robe and carried a shepherd's crook of gold.

He raised this aloft and a deathly silence fell on the assembly.

'Where are my sheep?'

The answer came from the crowd.

*'We are here, O Shepherd.'*

'Lift up your hearts with joy and thanksgiving. This is the Feast of Joy.'

*'The Feast of Joy and we are joyful.'*

'There shall be no more sorrow for you, no more pain. All is joy!'

*'All is joy…'*

'How many heads has the Shepherd?'

*'Three heads, a head of gold, a head of silver, a head of sounding brass.'*

'How many bodies have the Sheep?'

*'Three bodies, a body of flesh, a body of corruption, and a body of light.'*

'How shall you be sealed in the Flock?'

*'By the Sacrament of Blood.'*

'Are you prepared for that Sacrament?'

*'We are.'*

'Bind your eyes and hold forth your right arm.'

The crowd obediently bound their eyes with the green scarves provided for the purpose. Miss Carnaby, like the rest, held her arm out in front of her.

The Great Shepherd moved along the lines of his Flock. There were little cries, moans of either pain or ecstasy.

163

Miss Carnaby, to herself, said fiercely:

'Most blasphemous, the whole thing! This kind of religious hysteria is to be deplored. I shall remain absolutely calm and observe the reactions of other people. I will *not* be carried away—I will *not*...'

The Great Shepherd had come to her. She felt her arm taken, held, there was a sharp, stinging pain like the prick of a needle. The Shepherd's voice murmured:

'*The Sacrament of Blood that brings joy*...'

He passed on.

Presently there came a command.

'Unveil and enjoy the pleasures of the spirit!'

The sun was just sinking. Miss Carnaby looked round her. At one with the others, she moved slowly out of the Fold. She felt suddenly uplifted, happy. She sank down on a soft, grassy bank. Why had she ever thought she was a lonely, unwanted, middle-aged woman? Life was wonderful—she herself was wonderful! She had the power of thought—of dreaming. There was nothing that she could not accomplish!

A great rush of exhilaration surged through her. She observed her fellow devotees round her—they seemed suddenly to have grown to an immense stature.

'*Like trees walking*...' said Miss Carnaby to herself reverently.

She lifted her hand. It was a purposeful gesture—with it she could command the earth. Cæsar, Napoleon, Hitler—poor, miserable, little fellows! They knew nothing of what she, Amy Carnaby, could do! Tomorrow she would arrange for world peace, for International Brotherhood. There should be no more Wars—no more Poverty—no more Disease. She, Amy Carnaby, would design a New World.

But there need be no hurry. Time was infinite... Minute succeeded minute, hour succeeded hour! Miss Carnaby's limbs felt heavy, but her mind was delightfully free. It could roam at will over the whole universe. She slept—but even as she slept she dreamt... Great spaces... vast buildings... a new and wonderful world...

Gradually the world shrank, Miss Carnaby yawned. She moved her stiff limbs. What had happened since yesterday? Last night she had dreamt...

There was a moon. By it, Miss Carnaby could just distinguish the figures on her watch. To her stupefaction the hands pointed to a quarter to ten. The sun, as she knew, had set at eight-ten. Only an hour and thirty-five minutes ago? Impossible. And yet—

'*Very* remarkable,' said Miss Carnaby to herself.


Hercule Poirot said:

'You must obey my instructions very carefully. You understand?'

'Oh yes, M. Poirot. You may rely on me.'

'You have spoken of your intention to benefit the cult?'

'Yes, M. Poirot. I spoke to the Master—excuse me, to Dr Andersen myself. I told him very emotionally what a wonderful revelation the whole thing had been—how I had come to scoff and remained to believe. I—really it seemed quite natural to say all these things. Dr Andersen, you know, has a lot of magnetic charm.'

'So I perceive,' said Hercule Poirot drily.

'His manner was most convincing. One really feels he doesn't care about money at all. "Give what you can," he said smiling in that wonderful way of his, "if you can give nothing, it does not matter. You are one of the Flock just the same." "Oh, Dr Andersen," I said, "I am not so badly off as *that*. I have just inherited a considerable amount of money from a distant relative and though I cannot actually touch any of the money until the legal formalities are all complied with, there is one thing I want to do at once." And then I explained that I was making a will and that I wanted to leave all I had to the Brotherhood. I explained that I had no near relatives.'

'And he graciously accepted the bequest?'

'He was very detached about it. Said it would be many long years before I passed over, that he could tell I was cut out for a long life of joy and spiritual fulfilment. He really speaks most *movingly*.'

'So it would seem.'

Poirot's tone was dry. He went on:

'You mentioned your health?'

'Yes, M. Poirot. I told him that I had had lung trouble, and that it had recurred more than once, but that a final treatment in a Sanatorium some years ago had, I hoped, quite cured me.'

'Excellent!'

'Though why it is necessary for me to say that I am consumptive when my lungs are as sound as a bell I really cannot see.'

'Be assured it *is* necessary. You mentioned your friend?'

'Yes. I told him (strictly in confidence) that dear

Emmeline, besides the fortune she had inherited from her husband, would inherit an even larger sum shortly from an aunt who was deeply attached to her.'

'*Eh bien*, that ought to keep Mrs Clegg safe for the time being!'

'Oh, M. Poirot, do you really think there *is* anything wrong?'

'That is what I am going to endeavour to find out. Have you met a Mr Cole down at the Sanctuary?'

'There was a Mr Cole there last time I went down. A most peculiar man. He wears grass-green shorts and eats nothing but cabbage. He is a very ardent believer.'

'*Eh bien*, all progresses well—I make you my compliments on the work you have done—all is now set for the Autumn Festival.'

'Miss Carnaby—just a moment.'

Mr Cole clutched at Miss Carnaby, his eyes bright and feverish.

'I have had a Vision—a most remarkable Vision. I really must tell you about it.'

Miss Carnaby sighed. She was rather afraid of Mr Cole and his Visions. There were moments when she was decidedly of the opinion that Mr Cole was mad.

And she found these Visions of his sometimes very embarrassing. They recalled to her certain outspoken passages in that very modern German book on the Subconscious Mind which she had read before coming down to Devon.

Mr Cole, his eyes glistening, his lips twitching, began to talk excitedly.

'I had been meditating—reflecting on the Fullness of

Life, on the Supreme Joy of Oneness—and then, you know, my eyes were opened and I *saw*—'

Miss Carnaby braced herself and hoped that what Mr Cole had seen would not be what he had seen the last time—which had been, apparently, a Ritual Marriage in ancient Sumeria between a god and goddess.

'I saw'—Mr Cole leant towards her, breathing hard, his eyes looking (yes, really they did) *quite* mad—'the Prophet Elijah descending from Heaven in his fiery chariot.'

Miss Carnaby breathed a sigh of relief. Elijah was much better, she didn't mind Elijah.

'Below,' went on Mr Cole, 'were the altars of Baal—hundreds and hundreds of them. A Voice cried to me: "Look, write and testify that which you shall see—"'

He stopped and Miss Carnaby murmured politely: 'Yes?'

'On the altars were the sacrifices, bound there, help-less, waiting for the knife. Virgins—hundreds of vir-gins—young beautiful, naked virgins—'

Mr Cole smacked his lips, Miss Carnaby blushed.

'Then came the ravens, the ravens of Odin, flying from the North. They met the ravens of Elijah—together they circled in the sky—they swooped, they plucked out the eyes of the victims—there was wailing and gnashing of teeth—and the Voice cried: "Behold a Sacrifice—for on this day shall Jehovah and Odin sign blood brother-hood!" Then the Priests fell upon their victims, they raised their knives—they mutilated their victims—'

Desperately Miss Carnaby broke away from her tor-mentor who was now slavering at the mouth in a kind of sadistic fervour:

'Excuse me one moment.'

She hastily accosted Lipscomb, the man who occupied the Lodge which gave admission to Green Hills and who providentially happened to be passing.

'I wonder,' she said, 'if you have found a brooch of mine. I must have dropped it somewhere about the grounds.'

Lipscomb, who was a man immune from the general sweetness and light of Green Hills, merely growled that he hadn't seen any brooch. It wasn't *his* work to go about looking for things. He tried to shake off Miss Carnaby but she accompanied him, babbling about her brooch, till she had put a safe distance between herself and the fervour of Mr Cole.

At that moment, the Master himself came out of the Great Fold and, emboldened by his benignant smile, Miss Carnaby ventured to speak her mind to him.

Did he think that Mr Cole was quite—was quite—

The Master laid a hand on her shoulder.

'You must cast out Fear,' he said. 'Perfect Love casteth out Fear...'

'But I think Mr Cole *is* mad. Those Visions he has—'

'As yet,' said the Master, 'he sees Imperfectly... through the Glass of his own Carnal Nature. But the day will come when he shall see Spiritually—Face to Face.'

Miss Carnaby was abashed. Of course, put like that— She rallied to make a smaller protest.

'And really,' she said, 'need Lipscomb be so abominably rude?'

Again the Master gave his Heavenly Smile.

'Lipscomb,' he said, 'is a faithful watch-dog. He is a crude—a primitive soul—but faithful—utterly faithful.'

He strode on. Miss Carnaby saw him meet Mr Cole, pause, put a hand on Mr Cole's shoulder. She hoped that the Master's influence might alter the scope of future visions.

In any case, it was only a week now to the Autumn Festival.

On the afternoon preceding the Festival, Miss Carnaby met Hercule Poirot in a small teashop in the sleepy little town of Newton Woodbury. Miss Carnaby was flushed and even more breathless than usual. She sat sipping tea and crumbling a rock bun between her fingers.

Poirot asked several questions to which she replied monosyllabically.

Then he said:

'How many will there be at the Festival?'

'I think a hundred and twenty. Emmeline is there, of course, and Mr Cole—really *he* has been *very* odd lately. He has visions. He described some of them to me—really most peculiar—I hope, I do hope, he is not *insane*. Then there will be quite a lot of new members—nearly twenty.'

'Good. You know what you have to do?'

There was a moment's pause before Miss Carnaby said in a rather odd voice:

'I know what you told me, M. Poirot…'

'*Très bien!*'

Then Amy Carnaby said clearly and distinctly:

'*But I am not going to do it.*'

Hercule Poirot stared at her. Miss Carnaby rose to her feet. Her voice came fast and hysterical.

'You sent me here to spy on Dr Andersen. You suspected him of all sorts of things. But he is a wonderful man—a great Teacher. I believe in him heart and soul! And I am not going to do your spying work any more, M. Poirot! I am one of the Sheep of the Shepherd. The Master has a new message for the World and from now on, I belong to him body and soul. And I'll pay for my own tea, please.'

With which slight anticlimax Miss Carnaby plonked down one and threepence and rushed out of the tea-shop.

'*Nom d'un nom d'un nom,*' said Hercule Poirot.

The waitress had to ask him twice before he realized that she was presenting the bill. He met the interested stare of a surly looking man at the next table, flushed, paid the check and got up and went out.

He was thinking furiously.

Once again the Sheep were assembled in the Great Fold. The Ritual Questions and Answers had been chanted.

'Are you prepared for the Sacrament?'

'*We are.*'

'Bind your eyes and hold out your right arm.'

The Great Shepherd, magnificent in his green robe, moved along the waiting lines. The cabbage-eating, vision-seeing Mr Cole, next to Miss Carnaby, gave a gulp of painful ecstasy as the needle pierced his flesh.

The Great Shepherd stood by Miss Carnaby. His hands touched her arm...

'*No, you don't. None of that...*'

Words incredible—unprecedented. A scuffle, a roar of anger. Green veils were torn from eyes—to see an

171

unbelievable sight—the Great Shepherd struggling in the grasp of the sheep-skinned Mr Cole aided by another devotee.

In rapid professional tones, the erstwhile Mr Cole was saying:

'—and I have here a warrant for your arrest. I must warn you that anything you say may be used in evidence at your trial.'

There were other figures now at the door of the Sheep Fold—blue uniformed figures.

Someone cried: 'It's the *police*. They're taking the Master away. They're taking the Master…'

Everyone was shocked—horrified… to them the Great Shepherd was a martyr; suffering, as all great teachers suffer, from the ignorance and persecution of the outside world…

Meanwhile Detective Inspector Cole was carefully packing up the hypodermic syringe that had fallen from the Great Shepherd's hand.

'My brave colleague!'

Poirot shook Miss Carnaby warmly by the hand and introduced her to Chief Inspector Japp.

'First class work, Miss Carnaby,' said Chief Inspector Japp. 'We couldn't have done it without you and that's a fact.'

'Oh dear!' Miss Carnaby was flattered. 'It's so *kind* of you to say so. And I'm afraid, you know, that I've really *enjoyed* it all. The excitement, you know, and playing my part. I got quite carried away sometimes. I really felt I *was* one of those foolish women.'

'That's where your success lay,' said Japp. 'You were

172

the genuine article. Nothing less would have taken that gentleman in! He's a pretty astute scoundrel.'

Miss Carnaby turned to Poirot.

'That was a terrible moment in the teashop. I didn't know *what* to do. I just had to act on the spur of the moment.'

'You were magnificent,' said Poirot warmly. 'For a moment I thought that either you or I had taken leave of our senses. I thought for one little minute that you *meant* it.'

'It was such a shock,' said Miss Carnaby. 'Just when we had been talking confidentially. I saw in the glass that Lipscomb, who keeps the Lodge of the Sanctuary, was sitting at the table behind me. I don't know now if it was an accident or if he had actually followed me. As I say, I had to do the best I could on the spur of the minute and trust that you would understand.'

Poirot smiled.

'I did understand. There was only one person sitting near enough to overhear anything we said and as soon as I left the teashop I arranged to have him followed when he came out. When he went straight back to the Sanctuary I understood that I could rely on you and that you would not let me down—but I was afraid because it increased the danger for you.'

'Was—was there really danger? What was there in the syringe?'

Japp said:

'Will you explain, or shall I?'

Poirot said gravely:

'Mademoiselle, this Dr Andersen had perfected a scheme of exploitation and murder—scientific murder.

Most of his life has been spent in bacteriological research. Under a different name he has a chemical laboratory in Sheffield. There he makes cultures of various bacilli. It was his practice, at the Festivals, to inject into his followers a small but sufficient dose of Cannabis Indica—which is also known by the names of Hashish or Bhang. This gives delusions of grandeur and pleasurable enjoyment. It bound his devotees to him. These were the Spiritual Joys that he promised them.'

'Most remarkable,' said Miss Carnaby. 'Really a most remarkable sensation.'

Hercule Poirot nodded.

'That was his general stock in trade—a dominating personality, the power of creating mass hysteria and the reactions produced by this drug. But he had a second aim in view.

'Lonely women, in their gratitude and fervour, made wills leaving their money to the Cult. One by one, these women died. They died in their own homes and apparently of natural causes. Without being too technical I will try to explain. It is possible to make intensified cultures of certain bacteria. The bacillus Coli Communis, for instance, the cause of ulcerative colitis. Typhoid bacilli can be introduced into the system. So can the Pneumococcus. There is also what is termed Old Tuberculin which is harmless to a healthy person but which stimulates any old tubercular lesion into activity. You perceive the cleverness of the man? These deaths would occur in different parts of the country, with different doctors attending them and without any risk of arousing suspicion. He had also, I gather, cultivated a substance which had the power of delaying but intensifying the action of the chosen bacillus.'

'He's a devil, if there ever was one!' said Chief Inspector Japp.

Poirot went on:

'By my orders, you told him that you were a tuberculous subject. There was Old Tuberculin in the syringe when Cole arrested him. Since you were a healthy person it would not have harmed you, which is why I made you lay stress on your tubercular trouble. I was terrified that even now he *might* choose some other germ, but I respected your courage and I had to let you take the risk.'

'Oh, *that's* all right,' said Miss Carnaby brightly. 'I don't mind taking risks. I'm only frightened of bulls in fields and things like that. But have you enough evidence to *convict* this dreadful person?'

Japp grinned.

'Plenty of evidence,' he said. 'We've got his laboratory and his cultures and the whole layout!'

Poirot said:

'It is possible, I think, that he has committed a long line of murders. I may say that it was not because his mother was Jewish that he was dismissed from that German University. That merely made a convenient tale to account for his arrival here and to gain sympathy for him. Actually, I fancy, he is of pure Aryan blood.'

Miss Carnaby sighed.

'*Qu'est ce qu'il y a?*' asked Poirot.

'I was thinking,' said Miss Carnaby, 'of a marvellous dream I had at the First Festival—hashish, I suppose. I arranged the whole world so beautifully! No wars, no poverty, no ill health, no ugliness...'

'It must have been a fine dream,' said Japp enviously.

Miss Carnaby jumped up. She said:

'I must get home. Emily has been so anxious. And dear Augustus has been missing me terribly, I hear.'

Hercule Poirot said with a smile:

'He was afraid, perhaps, that like him, you were going "to die for Hercule Poirot"!'

# The Edge

Clare Halliwell walked down the short path that led from her cottage door to the gate. On her arm was a basket, and in the basket was a bottle of soup, some homemade jelly and a few grapes. There were not many poor people in the small village of Daymer's End, but such as there were were assiduously looked after, and Clare was one of the most efficient of the parish workers.

Clare Halliwell was thirty-two. She had an upright carriage, a healthy colour and nice brown eyes. She was not beautiful, but she looked fresh and pleasant and very English. Everybody liked her, and said she was a good sort. Since her mother's death, two years ago, she had lived alone in the cottage with her dog, Rover. She kept poultry and was fond of animals and of a healthy outdoor life.

As she unlatched the gate, a two-seater car swept past, and the driver, a girl in a red hat, waved a greeting. Clare responded, but for a moment her lips tightened. She felt that pang at her heart which always came when she saw Vivien Lee. Gerald's wife!

Medenham Grange, which lay just a mile outside the village, had belonged to the Lees for many generations. Sir Gerald Lee, the present owner of the Grange, was a man old for his years and considered by many stiff in manner. His pomposity really covered a good deal of shyness. He and Clare had played together as children. Later they had been friends, and a closer and dearer tie had been confidently expected by many—including, it may be said, Clare herself. There was no hurry, of course—but some day . . . She left it so in her own mind. Some day.

And then, just a year ago, the village had been startled by the news of Sir Gerald's marriage to a Miss Harper—a girl nobody had ever heard of!

The new Lady Lee had not been popular in the village. She took not the faintest interest in parochial matters, was bored by hunting, and loathed the country and outdoor sports. Many of the wiseacres shook their heads and wondered how it would end. It was easy to see where Sir Gerald's infatuation had come in. Vivien was a beauty. From head to foot she was a complete contrast to Clare Halliwell, small, elfin, dainty, with golden-red hair that curled enchantingly over her pretty ears, and big violet eyes that could shoot a sideways glance of provocation to the manner born.

Gerald Lee, in his simple man's way, had been anxious that his wife and Clare should be great friends. Clare was often asked to dine at the Grange, and Vivien made a pretty pretence of affectionate intimacy whenever they met. Hence that gay salutation of hers this morning.

Clare walked on and did her errand. The Vicar was also visiting the old woman in question and he and

Clare walked a few yards together afterwards before their ways parted. They stood still for a minute discussing parish affairs.

'Jones has broken out again, I'm afraid,' said the Vicar. 'And I had such hopes after he had volunteered, of his own accord, to take the pledge.'

'Disgusting,' said Clare crisply.

'It seems so to us,' said Mr Wilmot, 'but we must remember that it is very hard to put ourselves in his place and realize his temptation. The desire for drink is unaccountable to us, but we all have our own temptations, and thus we can understand.'

'I suppose we have,' said Clare uncertainly.

The Vicar glanced at her.

'Some of us have the good fortune to be very little tempted,' he said gently. 'But even to those people their hour comes. Watch and pray, remember, that ye enter not into temptation.'

Then bidding her goodbye, he walked briskly away. Clare went on thoughtfully, and presently she almost bumped into Sir Gerald Lee.

'Hullo, Clare. I was hoping to run across you. You look jolly fit. What a colour you've got.'

The colour had not been there a minute before. Lee went on:

'As I say, I was hoping to run across you. Vivien's got to go off to Bournemouth for the weekend. Her mother's not well. Can you dine with us Tuesday instead of tonight?'

'Oh, yes! Tuesday will suit me just as well.'

'That's all right, then. Splendid. I must hurry along.'

Clare went home to find her one faithful domestic standing on the doorstep looking out for her.

'There you are, Miss. Such a to-do. They've brought Rover home. He went off on his own this morning, and a car ran clean over him.'

Clare hurried to the dog's side. She adored animals, and Rover was her especial darling. She felt his legs one by one, and then ran her hands over his body. He groaned once or twice and licked her hand.

'If there's any serious injury, it's internal,' she said at last. 'No bones seem to be broken.'

'Shall we get the vet to see him, Miss?'

Clare shook her head. She had little faith in the local vet.

'We'll wait until tomorrow. He doesn't seem to be in great pain, and his gums are a good colour, so there can't be much internal bleeding. Tomorrow, if I don't like the look of him, I'll take him over to Skippington in the car and let Reeves have a look at him. He's far and away the best man.'

On the following day, Rover seemed weaker, and Clare duly carried out her project. The small town of Skippington was about forty miles away, a long run, but Reeves, the vet there, was celebrated for many miles round.

He diagnosed certain internal injuries, but held out good hopes of recovery, and Clare went away quite content to leave Rover in his charge.

There was only one hotel of any pretensions in Skippington, the *County Arms*. It was mainly frequented by commercial travellers, for there was no good hunting country near Skippington, and it was off the track of the main roads for motorists.

Lunch was not served till one o'clock, and as it wanted a few minutes of that hour, Clare amused herself by glancing over the entries in the open visitors' book.

Suddenly she gave a stifled exclamation. Surely she knew that handwriting, with its loops and whirls and flourishes? She had always considered it unmistakable. Even now she could have sworn—but of course it was clearly impossible. Vivien Lee was at Bournemouth. The entry itself showed it to be impossible:

Mr and Mrs Cyril Brown. London.

But in spite of herself her eyes strayed back again and again to that curly writing, and on an impulse she could not quite define she asked abruptly of the woman in the office:

'Mrs Cyril Brown? I wonder if that is the same one I know?'

'A small lady? Reddish hair? Very pretty. She came in a red two-seater car, madam. A Peugeot, I believe.'

Then it was! A coincidence would be too remarkable. As if in a dream, she heard the woman go on:

'They were here just over a month ago for a weekend, and liked it so much that they have come again. Newly married, I should fancy.'

Clare heard herself saying: 'Thank you. I don't think that could be my friend.'

Her voice sounded different, as though it belonged to someone else. Presently she was sitting in the dining-room, quietly eating cold roast beef, her mind a maze of conflicting thought and emotions.

She had no doubts whatever. She had summed Vivien

up pretty correctly on their first meeting. Vivien was that kind. She wondered vaguely who the man was. Someone Vivien had known before her marriage? Very likely—it didn't matter—nothing mattered, but Gerald.

What was she—Clare—to do about Gerald? He ought to know—surely he ought to know. It was clearly her duty to tell him. She had discovered Vivien's secret by accident, but she must lose no time in acquainting Gerald with the facts. She was Gerald's friend, not Vivien's.

But somehow or other she felt uncomfortable. Her conscience was not satisfied. On the face of it, her reasoning was good, but duty and inclination jumped suspiciously together. She admitted to herself that she disliked Vivien. Besides, if Gerald Lee were to divorce his wife—and Clare had no doubts at all that that was exactly what he would do, he was a man with an almost fanatical view of his own honour—then—well, the way would lie open for Gerald to come to her. Put like that, she shrank back fastidiously. Her own proposed action seemed naked and ugly.

The personal element entered in too much. She could not be sure of her own motives. Clare was essentially a high-minded, conscientious woman. She strove now very earnestly to see where her duty lay. She wished, as she had always wished, to do right. What was right in this case? What was wrong?

By a pure accident she had come into possession of facts that affected vitally the man she loved and the woman whom she disliked and—yes, one might as well be frank—of whom she was bitterly jealous. She could ruin that woman. Was she justified in doing so?

Clare had always held herself aloof from the backbiting and scandal which is an inevitable part of village life. She hated to feel that she now resembled one of those human ghouls she had always professed to despise.

Suddenly the Vicar's words that morning flashed across her mind:

'*Even to those people their hour comes.*'

Was this *her* hour? Was this *her* temptation? Had it come insidiously disguised as a duty? She was Clare Halliwell, a Christian, in love and charity with all men—and women. If she were to tell Gerald, she must be quite sure that only impersonal motives guided her. For the present she would say nothing.

She paid her bill for luncheon and drove away, feeling an indescribable lightening of spirit. Indeed, she felt happier than she had done for a long time. She felt glad that she had had the strength to resist temptation, to do nothing mean or unworthy. Just for a second it flashed across her mind that it might be a sense of power that had so lightened her spirits, but she dismissed the idea as fantastic.

By Tuesday night she was strengthened in her resolve. The revelation could not come through her. She must keep silence. Her own secret love for Gerald made speech impossible. Rather a high-minded view to take? Perhaps; but it was the only one possible for her.

She arrived at the Grange in her own little car. Sir Gerald's chauffeur was at the front door to drive it round to the garage after she had alighted, as the night was a wet one. He had just driven off when Clare remembered some books which she had borrowed and had brought with her to return. She called out, but the man did not hear her. The butler ran out after the car.

So, for a minute or two, Clare was alone in the hall, close to the door of the drawing-room which the butler had just unlatched prior to announcing her. Those inside the room, however, knew nothing of her arrival, and so it was that Vivien's voice, high pitched—not quite the voice of a lady—rang out clearly and distinctly.

'Oh, we're only waiting for Clare Halliwell. You must know her—lives in the village—supposed to be one of the local belles, but frightfully unattractive really. She tried her best to catch Gerald, but he wasn't having any.

'Oh, yes, darling'—this in answer to a murmured protest from her husband. 'She did—you mayn't be aware of the fact—but she did her very utmost. Poor old Clare! A good sort, but such a dump!'

Clare's face went dead white, her hands, hanging against her sides, clenched themselves in anger such as she had never known before. At that moment she could have murdered Vivien Lee. It was only by a supreme physical effort that she regained control of herself. That, and the half-formed thought that she held it in her power to punish Vivien for those cruel words.

The butler had returned with the books. He opened the door, announced her, and in another moment she was greeting a roomful of people in her usual pleasant manner.

Vivien, exquisitely dressed in some dark wine colour that showed off her white fragility, was particularly affectionate and gushing. They didn't see half enough of Clare. She, Vivien, was going to learn golf, and Clare must come out with her on the links.

184

Gerald was very attentive and kind. Though he had no suspicion that she had overheard his wife's words, he had some vague idea of making up for them. He was very fond of Clare, and he wished Vivien wouldn't say the things she did. He and Clare had been friends, nothing more—and if there was an uneasy suspicion at the back of his mind that he was shirking the truth in that last statement, he put it away from him.

After dinner the talk fell on dogs, and Clare recounted Rover's accident. She purposely waited for a lull in the conversation to say:

'. . . so, on Saturday, I took him to Skippington.'

She heard the sudden rattle of Vivien Lee's coffee-cup on the saucer, but she did not look at her—yet.

'To see that man, Reeves?'

'Yes. He'll be all right, I think. I had lunch at the *County Arms* afterwards. Rather a decent little pub.' She turned now to Vivien. 'Have you ever stayed there?'

If she had had any doubts, they were swept aside. Vivien's answer came quick—in stammering haste.

'I? Oh! N-no, no.'

Fear was in her eyes. They were wide and dark with it, as they met Clare's. Clare's eyes told nothing. They were calm, scrutinizing. No one could have dreamt of the keen pleasure that they veiled. At that moment Clare almost forgave Vivien for the words she had overheard earlier in the evening. She tasted in that moment a fullness of power that almost made her head reel. She held Vivien Lee in the hollow of her hand.

The following day, she received a note from the other woman. Would Clare come up and have tea with her quietly that afternoon? Clare refused.

Then Vivien called on her. Twice she came at hours when Clare was almost certain to be at home. On the first occasion, Clare really was out; on the second, she slipped out by the back way when she saw Vivien coming up the path.

'She's not sure yet whether I know or not,' she said to herself. 'She wants to find out without committing herself. But she shan't—not until I'm ready.'

Clare hardly knew herself what she was waiting for. She had decided to keep silence—that was the only straight and honourable course. She felt an additional glow of virtue when she remembered the extreme provocation she had received. After overhearing the way Vivien talked of her behind her back, a weaker character, she felt, might have abandoned her good resolutions.

She went twice to church on Sunday. First to early Communion, from which she came out strengthened and uplifted. No personal feelings should weigh with her—nothing mean or petty. She went again to morning service. Mr Wilmot preached on the famous prayer of the Pharisee. He sketched the life of that man, a good man, pillar of the church. And he pictured the slow, creeping blight of spiritual pride that distorted and soiled all that he was.

Clare did not listen very attentively. Vivien was in the big square pew of the Lee family, and Clare knew by instinct that the other intended to get hold of her afterwards.

So it fell out. Vivien attached herself to Clare, walked home with her, and asked if she might come in. Clare, of course, assented. They sat in Clare's little sitting-room, bright with flowers and old-fashioned chintzes. Vivien's talk was desultory and jerky.

'I was at Bournemouth, you know, last weekend,' she remarked presently.

'Gerald told me so,' said Clare.

They looked at each other. Vivien appeared almost plain today. Her face had a sharp, foxy look that robbed it of much of its charm.

'When you were at Skippington—' began Vivien.

'When I was at Skippington?' echoed Clare politely.

'You were speaking about some little hotel there.'

'The *County Arms*. Yes. You didn't know it, you said?'

'I—I have been there once.'

'Oh!'

She had only to keep still and wait. Vivien was quite unfitted to bear a strain of any kind. Already she was breaking down under it. Suddenly she leant forward and spoke vehemently.

'You don't like me. You never have. You've always hated me. You're enjoying yourself now, playing with me like a cat with a mouse. You're cruel—cruel. That's why I'm afraid of you, because deep down you're cruel.'

'Really, Vivien!' said Clare sharply.

'You *know*, don't you? Yes, I can see that you know. You knew that night—when you spoke about Skippington. You've found out somehow. Well, I want to know what you are going to do about it? What are you going to do?'

Clare did not reply for a minute, and Vivien sprang to her feet.

'What are you going to do? I must know. You're not going to deny that you know all about it?'

'I do not propose to deny anything,' said Clare coldly.

'You saw me there that day?'

'No. I saw your handwriting in the book—Mr and Mrs Cyril Brown.'

Vivien flushed darkly.

'Since then,' continued Clare quietly, 'I have made inquiries. I find that you were not at Bournemouth that weekend. Your mother never sent for you. Exactly the same thing happened about six weeks previously.'

Vivien sank down again on the sofa. She burst into furious crying, the crying of a frightened child.

'What are you going to do?' she gasped. 'Are you going to tell Gerald?'

'I don't know yet,' said Clare.

She felt calm, omnipotent.

Vivien sat up, pushing the red curls back from her forehead.

'Would you like to hear all about it?'

'It would be as well, I think.'

Vivien poured out the whole story. There was no reticence in her. Cyril 'Brown' was Cyril Haviland, a young engineer to whom she had previously been engaged. His health failed, and he lost his job, whereupon he made no bones about jilting the penniless Vivien and marrying a rich widow many years older than himself. Soon afterwards Vivien married Gerald Lee.

She had met Cyril again by chance. That was the first of many meetings. Cyril, backed by his wife's money, was prospering in his career, and becoming a well-known figure. It was a sordid story, a story of backstairs meeting, of ceaseless lying and intrigue.

'I love him so,' Vivien repeated again and again, with

a sudden moan, and each time the words made Clare feel physically sick.

At last the stammering recital came to an end. Vivien muttered a shamefaced: 'Well?'

'What am I going to do?' asked Clare. 'I can't tell you. I must have time to think.'

'You won't give me away to Gerald?'

'It may be my duty to do so.'

'No, no.' Vivien's voice rose to a hysterical shriek. 'He'll divorce me. He won't listen to a word. He'll find out from that hotel, and Cyril will be dragged into it. And then his wife will divorce him. Everything will go—his career, his health—he'll be penniless again. He'd never forgive me—never.'

'If you'll excuse my saying so,' said Clare, 'I don't think much of this Cyril of yours.'

Vivien paid no attention.

'I tell you he'll hate me—hate me. I can't bear it. Don't tell Gerald. I'll do anything you like, but don't tell Gerald.'

'I must have time to decide,' said Clare gravely. 'I can't promise anything off-hand. In the meantime, you and Cyril mustn't meet again.'

'No, no, we won't. I swear it.'

'When I know what's the right thing to do,' said Clare, 'I'll let you know.'

She got up. Vivien went out of the house in a furtive, slinking way, glancing back over her shoulder.

Clare wrinkled her nose in disgust. A beastly affair. Would Vivien keep her promise not to see Cyril? Probably not. She was weak—rotten all through.

That afternoon Clare went for a long walk. There

was a path which led along the downs. On the left the green hills sloped gently down to the sea far below, while the path wound steadily upward. This walk was known locally as the Edge. Though safe enough if you kept to the path, it was dangerous to wander from it. Those insidious gentle slopes were dangerous. Clare had lost a dog there once. The animal had gone racing over the smooth grass, gaining momentum, had been unable to stop and had gone over the edge of the cliff to be dashed to pieces on the sharp rocks below.

The afternoon was clear and beautiful. From far below there came the ripple of the sea, a soothing murmur. Clare sat down on the short green turf and stared out over the blue water. She must face this thing clearly. What did she mean to do?

She thought of Vivien with a kind of disgust. How the girl had crumpled up, how abjectly she had surrendered! Clare felt a rising contempt. She had no pluck—no grit.

Nevertheless, much as she disliked Vivien, Clare decided that she would continue to spare her for the present. When she got home she wrote a note to her, saying that although she could make no definite promise for the future, she had decided to keep silence for the present.

Life went on much the same in Daymer's End. It was noticed locally that Lady Lee was looking far from well. On the other hand, Clare Halliwell bloomed. Her eyes were brighter, she carried her head higher, and there was a new confidence and assurance in her manner. She and Lady Lee often met, and it was noticed on these occasions that the younger woman watched the older with a flattering attention to her slightest word.

Sometimes Miss Halliwell would make remarks that seemed a little ambiguous—not entirely relevant to the matter in hand. She would suddenly say that she had changed her mind about many things lately—that it was curious how a little thing might alter one's point of view entirely. One was apt to give way too much to pity—and that was really quite wrong.

When she said things of that kind she usually looked at Lady Lee in a peculiar way, and the latter would suddenly grow quite white, and look almost terrified.

But as the year drew on, these little subtleties became less apparent. Clare continued to make the same remarks, but Lady Lee seemed less affected by them. She began to recover her looks and spirits. Her old gay manner returned.

One morning, when she was taking her dog for a walk, Clare met Gerald in a lane. The latter's spaniel fraternized with Rover, while his master talked to Clare.

'Heard our news?' he said buoyantly. 'I expect Vivien's told you.'

'What sort of news? Vivien hasn't mentioned anything in particular.'

'We're going abroad—for a year—perhaps longer. Vivien's fed up with this place. She never has cared for it, you know.' He sighed, for a moment or two he looked downcast. Gerald Lee was very proud of his home. 'Anyway, I've promised her a change. I've taken a villa near Algiers. A wonderful place, by all accounts.' He laughed a little self-consciously. 'Quite a second honeymoon, eh?'

For a minute or two Clare could not speak. Something seemed rising up in her throat and suffocating her.

She could see the white walls of the villa, the orange trees, smell the soft perfumed breath of the South. A second honeymoon!

They were going to escape. Vivien no longer believed in her threats. She was going away, care-free, gay, happy.

Clare heard her own voice, a little hoarse in timbre, saying the appropriate things. How lovely! She envied them!

Mercifully at that moment Rover and the spaniel decided to disagree. In the scuffle that ensued further conversation was out of the question.

That afternoon Clare sat down and wrote a note to Vivien. She asked her to meet her on the Edge the following day, as she had something very important to say to her.

The next morning dawned bright and cloudless. Clare walked up the steep path of the Edge with a lightened heart. What a perfect day! She was glad that she had decided to say what had to be said out in the open, under the blue sky, instead of in her stuffy little sitting-room. She was sorry for Vivien, very sorry indeed, but the thing had got to be done.

She saw a yellow dot, like some yellow flower higher up by the side of the path. As she came nearer it resolved itself into the figure of Vivien, dressed in a yellow knitted frock, sitting on the short turf, her hands clasped round her knees.

'Good morning,' said Clare. 'Isn't it a perfect morning?'

'Is it?' said Vivien. 'I haven't noticed. What was it you wanted to say to me?'

Clare dropped down on the grass beside her.

192

'I'm quite out of breath,' she said apologetically. 'It's a steep pull up here.'

'Damn you!' cried Vivien shrilly. 'Why can't you say it, you smooth-faced devil, instead of torturing me?'

Clare looked shocked, and Vivien hastily recanted.

'I didn't mean that. I'm sorry, Clare. I am indeed. Only—my nerves are all to pieces, and your sitting here and talking about the weather—well, it got me all rattled.'

'You'll have a nervous breakdown if you're not careful,' said Clare coldly.

Vivien gave a short laugh.

'Go over the edge? No—I'm not that kind. I'll never be a loony. Now tell me—what's all this about?'

Clare was silent for a moment, then she spoke, looking not at Vivien, but steadily out over the sea.

'I thought it only fair to warn you that I can no longer keep silence about—about what happened last year.'

'You mean—you'll go to Gerald with the whole story?'

'Unless you'll tell him yourself. That would be infinitely the better way.'

Vivien laughed sharply.

'You know well enough I haven't got the pluck to do that.'

Clare did not contradict the assertion. She had had proof before of Vivien's utterly craven temper.

'It would be infinitely better,' she repeated.

Again Vivien gave that short, ugly laugh.

'It's your precious conscience, I suppose, that drives you to do this?' she sneered.

'I dare say it seems very strange to you,' said Clare quietly. 'But it honestly is that.'

Vivien's white, set face stared into hers.

'My God!' she said. 'I really believe you mean it, too. You actually think that's the reason.'

'It *is* the reason.'

'No, it isn't. If so, you'd have done it before—long ago. Why didn't you? No, don't answer. I'll tell you. You got more pleasure out of holding it over me—that's why. You liked to keep me on tenterhooks, and make me wince and squirm. You'd say things—diabolical things—just to torment me and keep me perpetually on the jump. And so they did for a bit—till I got used to them.'

'You got to feel secure,' said Clare.

'You saw that, didn't you? But even then, you held back, enjoying your sense of power. But now we're going away, escaping from you, perhaps even going to be happy—you couldn't stick that at any price. So your convenient conscience wakes up!'

She stopped, panting. Clare said, still very quietly:

'I can't prevent your saying all these fantastical things; but I can assure you they're not true.'

Vivien turned suddenly and caught her by the hand.

'Clare—for God's sake! I've been straight—I've done what you said. I've not seen Cyril again—I swear it.'

'That's nothing to do with it.'

'Clare—haven't you any pity—any kindness? I'll go down on my knees to you.'

'Tell Gerald yourself. If you tell him, he may forgive you.'

Vivien laughed scornfully.

'You know Gerald better than that. He'll be rabid—vindictive. He'll make me suffer—he'll make Cyril suffer. That's what I can't bear. Listen, Clare—he's doing so well. He's invented something—machinery, I don't understand about it, but it may be a wonderful success. He's working it out now—his wife supplies the money for it, of course. But she's suspicious—jealous. If she finds out, and she will find out if Gerald starts proceedings for divorce—she'll chuck Cyril—his work, everything. Cyril will be ruined.'

'I'm not thinking of Cyril,' said Clare. 'I'm thinking of Gerald. Why don't you think a little of him, too?'

'Gerald! I don't care that—' she snapped her fingers 'for Gerald. I never have. We might as well have the truth now we're at it. But I do care for Cyril. I'm a rotter, through and through, I admit it. I dare say he's a rotter, too. But my feeling for him—that *isn't* rotten. I'd die for him, do you hear? I'd die for him!'

'That is easily said,' said Clare derisively.

'You think I'm not in earnest? Listen, if you go on with this beastly business, I'll kill myself. Sooner than have Cyril brought into it and ruined, I'd do that.'

Clare remained unimpressed.

'You don't believe me?' said Vivien, panting.

'Suicide needs a lot of courage.'

Vivien flinched back as though she had been struck.

'You've got me there. Yes, I've no pluck. If there were an easy way—'

'There's an easy way in front of you,' said Clare. 'You've only got to run straight down that green slope. It would be all over in a couple of minutes. Remember that child last year.'

'Yes,' said Vivien thoughtfully. 'That would be easy—quite easy—if one really wanted to—'

Clare laughed.

Vivien turned to her.

'Let's have this out once more. Can't you see that by keeping silence as long as you have, you've—you've no right to go back on it now? I'll not see Cyril again. I'll be a good wife to Gerald—I swear I will. Or I'll go away and never see him again? Whichever you like. Clare—'

Clare got up.

'I advise you,' she said, 'to tell your husband yourself . . . otherwise—I shall.'

'I see,' said Vivien softly. 'Well, I can't let Cyril suffer . . .' She got up, stood still as though considering for a minute or two, then ran lightly down to the path, but instead of stopping, crossed it and went down the slope. Once she half turned her head and waved a hand gaily to Clare, then she ran on gaily, lightly, as a child might run, out of sight . . .

Clare stood petrified. Suddenly she heard cries, shouts, a clamour of voices. Then—silence.

She picked her way stiffly down to the path. About a hundred yards away a party of people coming up it had stopped. They were staring and pointing. Clare ran down and joined them.

'Yes, Miss, someone's fallen over the cliff. Two men have gone down—to see.'

She waited. Was it an hour, or eternity, or only a few minutes?

A man came toiling up the ascent. It was the Vicar in his shirt sleeves. His coat had been taken off to cover what lay below.

'Horrible,' he said, his face was very white. 'Mercifully death must have been instantaneous.'

He saw Clare, and came over to her.

'This must have been a terrible shock to you. You were taking a walk together, I understand?'

Clare heard herself answering mechanically.

Yes. They had just parted. No, Lady Lee's manner had been quite normal. One of the group interposed the information that the lady was laughing and waving her hand. A terribly dangerous place—there ought to be a railing along the path.

The Vicar's voice rose again.

'An accident—yes, clearly an accident.'

And then suddenly Clare laughed—a hoarse, raucous laugh that echoed along the cliff.

'*That's a damned lie,*' she said. '*I killed her.*'

She felt someone patting her shoulder, a voice spoke soothingly.

'There, there. It's all right. You'll be all right presently.'

But Clare was not all right presently. She was never all right again. She persisted in the delusion—certainly a delusion, since at least eight persons had witnessed the scene—that she had killed Vivien Lee.

She was very miserable till Nurse Lauriston came to take charge. Nurse Lauriston was very successful with mental cases.

'Humour them, poor things,' she would say comfortably.

So she told Clare that she was a wardress from Pentonville Prison. Clare's sentence, she said, had been commuted to penal servitude for life. A room was fitted up as a cell.

'And now, I think, we shall be quite happy and comfortable,' said Nurse Lauriston to the doctor. 'Round-bladed knives if you like, doctor, but I don't think there's the least fear of suicide. She's not the type. Too self-centred. Funny how those are often the ones who go over the edge most easily.'

# The Blood-Stained Pavement

'It's curious,' said Joyce Lemprière, 'but I hardly like telling you my story. It happened a long time ago—five years ago to be exact—but it's sort of haunted me ever since. The smiling, bright, top part of it—and the hidden gruesomeness underneath. And the queer thing is that the sketch I painted at the time has become tinged with the same atmosphere. When you look at it first it is just a rough sketch of a little steep Cornish street with the sunlight on it. But if you look long enough at it something sinister creeps in. I have never sold it but I never look at it. It lives in the studio in a corner with its face to the wall.

'The name of the place was Rathole. It is a queer little Cornish fishing village, very picturesque—too picturesque perhaps. There is rather too much of the atmosphere of "Ye Olde Cornish Tea House" about it. It has shops with bobbed-headed girls in smocks doing hand-illuminated mottoes on parchment. It is pretty and it is quaint, but it is very self-consciously so.'

'Don't I know,' said Raymond West, groaning. 'The curse of the charabanc, I suppose. No matter how narrow the lanes leading down to them no picturesque village is safe.'

Joyce nodded.

'They are narrow lanes that lead down to Rathole and very steep, like the side of a house. Well, to get on with my story. I had come down to Cornwall for a fortnight, to sketch. There is an old inn in Rathole, The Polharwith Arms. It was supposed to be the only house left standing by the Spaniards when they shelled the place in fifteen hundred and something.'

'Not shelled,' said Raymond West, frowning. 'Do try to be historically accurate, Joyce.'

'Well, at all events they landed guns somewhere along the coast and they fired them and the houses fell down. Anyway that is not the point. The inn was a wonderful old place with a kind of porch in front built on four pillars. I got a very good pitch and was just settling down to work when a car came creeping and twisting down the hill. Of course, it *would* stop before the inn—just where it was most awkward for me. The people got out—a man and a woman—I didn't notice them particularly. She had a kind of mauve linen dress on and a mauve hat.

'Presently the man came out again and to my great thankfulness drove the car down to the quay and left it there. He strolled back past me towards the inn. Just at that moment another beastly car came twisting down, and a woman got out of it dressed in the brightest chintz frock I have ever seen, scarlet poinsettias, I think they were, and she had on one of those big native straw hats—Cuban, aren't they?—in very bright scarlet.

'This woman didn't stop in front of the inn but drove the car farther down the street towards the other one.

Then she got out and the man seeing her gave an astonished shout. "Carol," he cried, "in the name of all that is wonderful. Fancy meeting you in this out-of-the-way spot. I haven't seen you for years. Hello, there's Margery—my wife, you know. You must come and meet her."

'They went up the street towards the inn side by side, and I saw the other woman had just come out of the door and was moving down towards them. I had had just a glimpse of the woman called Carol as she passed by me. Just enough to see a very white powdered chin and a flaming scarlet mouth and I wondered—I just wondered—if Margery would be so very pleased to meet her. I hadn't seen Margery near to, but in the distance she looked dowdy and extra prim and proper.

'Well, of course, it was not any of my business but you get very queer little glimpses of life sometimes, and you can't help speculating about them. From where they were standing I could just catch fragments of their conversation that floated down to me. They were talking about bathing. The husband, whose name seemed to be Denis, wanted to take a boat and row round the coast. There was a famous cave well worth seeing, so he said, about a mile along. Carol wanted to see the cave too but suggested walking along the cliffs and seeing it from the land side. She said she hated boats. In the end they fixed it that way. Carol was to go along the cliff path and meet them at the cave, and Denis and Margery would take a boat and row round.

'Hearing them talk about bathing made me want to bathe too. It was a very hot morning and I wasn't doing particularly good work. Also, I fancied that the afternoon sunlight would be far more attractive in effect. So

I packed up my things and went off to a little beach that I knew of—it was quite the opposite direction from the cave, and was rather a discovery of mine. I had a ripping bathe there and I lunched off a tinned tongue and two tomatoes, and I came back in the afternoon full of confidence and enthusiasm to get on with my sketch.

'The whole of Rathole seemed to be asleep. I had been right about the afternoon sunlight, the shadows were far more telling. The Polharwith Arms was the principal note of my sketch. A ray of sunlight came slanting obliquely down and hit the ground in front of it and had rather a curious effect. I gathered that the bathing party had returned safely, because two bathing dresses, a scarlet one and a dark blue one, were hanging from the balcony, drying in the sun.

'Something had gone a bit wrong with one corner of my sketch and I bent over it for some moments doing something to put it right. When I looked up again there was a figure leaning against one of the pillars of The Polharwith Arms, who seemed to have appeared there by magic. He was dressed in seafaring clothes and was, I suppose, a fisherman. But he had a long dark beard, and if I had been looking for a model for a wicked Spanish captain I couldn't have imagined anyone better. I got to work with feverish haste before he should move away, though from his attitude he looked as though he was pefectly prepared to prop up the pillars through all eternity.

'He did move, however, but luckily not until I had got what I wanted. He came over to me and he began to talk. Oh, how that man talked.

'"Rathole," he said, "was a very interesting place."

202

'I knew that already but although I said so that didn't save me. I had the whole history of the shelling—I mean the destroying—of the village, and how the landlord of the Polharwith Arms was the last man to be killed. Run through on his own threshold by a Spanish captain's sword, and of how his blood spurted out on the pavement and no one could wash out the stain for a hundred years.

'It all fitted in very well with the languorous drowsy feeling of the afternoon. The man's voice was very suave and yet at the same time there was an undercurrent in it of something rather frightening. He was very obsequious in his manner, yet I felt underneath he was cruel. He made me understand the Inquisition and the terrors of all the things the Spaniards did better than I have ever done before.

'All the time he was talking to me I went on painting, and suddenly I realized that in the excitement of listening to his story I had painted in something that was not there. On that white square of pavement where the sun fell before the door of The Polharwith Arms, I had painted in bloodstains. It seemed extraordinary that the mind could play such tricks with the hand, but as I looked over towards the inn again I got a second shock. My hand had only painted what my eyes saw—drops of blood on the white pavement.

'I stared for a minute or two. Then I shut my eyes, said to myself, "Don't be so stupid, there's nothing there, really," then I opened them again, but the bloodstains were still there.

'I suddenly felt I couldn't stand it. I interrupted the fisherman's flood of language.

"'Tell me,' I said, "my eyesight is not very good. Are those bloodstains on that pavement over there?"

'He looked at me indulgently and kindly.

"'No bloodstains in these days, lady. What I am telling you about is nearly five hundred years ago."

"'Yes," I said, "but now—on the pavement"—the words died away in my throat. I *knew—I knew* that he wouldn't see what I was seeing. I got up and with shaking hands began to put my things together. As I did so the young man who had come in the car that morning came out of the inn door. He looked up and down the street perplexedly. On the balcony above his wife came out and collected the bathing things. He walked down towards the car but suddenly swerved and came across the road towards the fisherman.

"'Tell me, my man,' he said. "You don't know whether the lady who came in that second car there has got back yet?"

"'Lady in a dress with flowers all over it? No, sir, I haven't seen her. She went along the cliff towards the cave this morning."

"'I know, I know. We all bathed there together, and then she left us to walk home and I have not seen her since. It can't have taken her all this time. The cliffs round here are not dangerous, are they?"

"'It depends, sir, on the way you go. The best way is to take a man what knows the place with you."

'He very clearly meant himself and was beginning to enlarge on the theme, but the young man cut him short unceremoniously and ran back towards the inn calling up to his wife on the balcony.

"'I say, Margery, Carol hasn't come back yet. Odd, isn't it?"

'I didn't hear Margery's reply, but her husband went on. "Well, we can't wait any longer. We have got to push on to Penrithar. Are you ready? I will turn the car."

'He did as he had said, and presently the two of them drove off together. Meanwhile I had deliberately been nerving myself to prove how ridiculous my fancies were. When the car had gone I went over to the inn and examined the pavement closely. Of course there were no bloodstains there. No, all along it had been the result of my distorted imagination. Yet, somehow, it seemed to make the thing more frightening. It was while I was standing there that I heard the fisherman's voice.

'He was looking at me curiously. "You thought you saw bloodstains here, eh, lady?"

'I nodded.

"'That is very curious, that is very curious. We have got a superstition here, lady. If anyone sees those blood-stains—"

'He paused.

"'Well?" I said.

'He went on in his soft voice, Cornish in intonation, but unconsciously smooth and well-bred in its pronunciation, and completely free from Cornish turns of speech.

"'They do say, lady, that if anyone sees those blood-stains that there will be a death within twenty-four hours."

'Creepy! It gave me a nasty feeling all down my spine.

'He went on persuasively. "There is a very interesting tablet in the church, lady, about a death—"

205

'"No thanks," I said decisively, and I turned sharply on my heel and walked up the street towards the cottage where I was lodging. Just as I got there I saw in the distance the woman called Carol coming along the cliff path. She was hurrying. Against the grey of the rocks she looked like some poisonous scarlet flower. Her hat was the colour of blood . . .

'I shook myself. Really, I had blood on the brain.

'Later I heard the sound of her car. I wondered whether she too was going to Penrithar; but she took the road to the left in the opposite direction. I watched the car crawl up the hill and disappear, and I breathed somehow more easily. Rathole seemed its quiet sleepy self once more.'

'If that is all,' said Raymond West as Joyce came to a stop, 'I will give my verdict at once. Indigestion, spots before the eyes after meals.'

'It isn't all,' said Joyce. 'You have got to hear the sequel. I read it in the paper two days later under the heading of "Sea Bathing Fatality". It told how Mrs Dacre, the wife of Captain Denis Dacre, was unfortunately drowned at Landeer Cove, just a little farther along the coast. She and her husband were staying at the time at the hotel there, and had declared their intention of bathing, but a cold wind sprang up. Captain Dacre had declared it was too cold, so he and some other people in the hotel had gone off to the golf links near by. Mrs Dacre, however, had said it was not too cold for her and she went off alone down to the cove. As she didn't return her husband became alarmed, and in company with his friends went down to the beach. They found her clothes lying beside a rock, but no trace of the

206

unfortunate lady. Her body was not found until nearly a week later when it was washed ashore at a point some distance down the coast. There was a bad blow on her head which had occurred before death, and the theory was that she must have dived into the sea and hit her head on a rock. As far as I could make out her death would have occurred just twenty-four hours after the time I saw the bloodstains.'

'I protest,' said Sir Henry. 'This is not a problem—this is a ghost story. Miss Lemprière is evidently a medium.'

Mr Petherick gave his usual cough.

'One point strikes me—' he said, 'that blow on the head. We must not, I think, exclude the possibility of foul play. But I do not see that we have any data to go upon. Miss Lemprière's hallucination, or vision, is interesting certainly, but I do not see clearly the point on which she wishes us to pronounce.'

'Indigestion and coincidence,' said Raymond, 'and anyway you can't be sure that they were the same people. Besides, the curse, or whatever it was, would only apply to the actual inhabitants of Rathole.'

'I feel,' said Sir Henry, 'that the sinister seafaring man has something to do with this tale. But I agree with Mr Petherick, Miss Lemprière has given us very little data.'

Joyce turned to Dr Pender who smilingly shook his head.

'It is a most interesting story,' he said, 'but I am afraid I agree with Sir Henry and Mr Petherick that there is very little data to go upon.'

Joyce then looked curiously at Miss Marple, who smiled back at her.

'I, too, think you are just a little unfair, Joyce dear,' she said. 'Of course, it is different for me. I mean, we, being women, appreciate the point about clothes. I don't think it is a fair problem to put to a man. It must have meant a lot of rapid changing. What a wicked woman! And a still more wicked man.'

Joyce stared at her.

'Aunt Jane,' she said. 'Miss Marple, I mean, I believe—I do really believe you know the truth.'

'Well, dear,' said Miss Marple, 'it is much easier for me sitting here quietly than it was for you—and being an artist you are so susceptible to atmosphere, aren't you? Sitting here with one's knitting, one just sees the facts. Bloodstains dropped on the pavement from the bathing dress hanging above, and being a red bathing dress, of course, the criminals themselves did not realize it was bloodstained. Poor thing, poor young thing!'

'Excuse me, Miss Marple,' said Sir Henry, 'but you do know that I am entirely in the dark still. You and Miss Lemprière seem to know what you are talking about, but we men are still in utter darkness.'

'I will tell you the end of the story now,' said Joyce. 'It was a year later. I was at a little east coast seaside resort, and I was sketching, when suddenly I had that queer feeling one has of something having happened before. There were two people, a man and a woman, on the pavement in front of me, and they were greeting a third person, a woman dressed in a scarlet poinsettia chintz dress. "Carol, by all that is wonderful! Fancy meeting you after all these years. You don't know my wife? Joan, this is an old friend of mine, Miss Harding."

'I recognized the man at once. It was the same Denis

I had seen at Rathole. The wife was different—that is, she was a Joan instead of a Margery; but she was the same type, young and rather dowdy and very inconspicuous. I thought for a minute I was going mad. They began to talk of going bathing. I will tell you what I did. I marched straight then and there to the police station. I thought they would probably think I was off my head, but I didn't care. And as it happened everything was quite all right. There was a man from Scotland Yard there, and he had come down just about this very thing. It seems—oh, it's horrible to talk about—that the police had got suspicions of Denis Dacre. That wasn't his real name—he took different names on different occasions. He got to know girls, usually quiet inconspicuous girls without many relatives or friends, he married them and insured their lives for large sums and then—oh, it's horrible! The woman called Carol was his real wife, and they always carried out the same plan. That is really how they came to catch him. The insurance companies became suspicious. He would come to some quiet seaside place with his new wife, then the other woman would turn up and they would all go bathing together. Then the wife would be murdered and Carol would put on her clothes and go back in the boat with him. Then they would leave the place, wherever it was, after inquiring for the supposed Carol and when they got outside the village Carol would hastily change back into her own flamboyant clothes and her vivid make-up and would go back there and drive off in her own car. They would find out which way the current was flowing and the supposed death would take place at the next bathing place along the coast that way. Carol would play the part

209

of the wife and would go down to some lonely beach and would leave the wife's clothes there by a rock and depart in her flowery chintz dress to wait quietly until her husband could rejoin her.

'I suppose when they killed poor Margery some of the blood must have spurted over Carol's bathing suit, and being a red one they didn't notice it, as Miss Marple says. But when they hung it over the balcony it dripped. Ugh!' she gave a shiver. 'I can see it still.'

'Of course,' said Sir Henry, 'I remember very well now. Davis was the man's real name. It had quite slipped my memory that one of his many aliases was Dacre. They were an extraordinarily cunning pair. It always seemed so amazing to me that no one spotted the change of identity. I suppose, as Miss Marple says, clothes are more easily identified than faces; but it was a very clever scheme, for although we suspected Davis it was not easy to bring the crime home to him as he always seemed to have an unimpeachable alibi.'

'Aunt Jane,' said Raymond, looking at her curiously, 'how do you do it? You have lived such a peaceful life and yet nothing seems to surprise you.'

'I always find one thing very like another in this world,' said Miss Marple. 'There was Mrs Green, you know, she buried five children—and every one of them insured. Well, naturally, one began to get suspicious.'

She shook her head.

'There is a great deal of wickedness in village life. I hope you dear young people will never realize how very wicked the world is.'

# The Adventure of
# the Dartmoor Bungalow

'But where are we going?' I inquired for about the tenth time.

Poirot loves being mysterious. He will never part with a piece of information until the last possible moment. In this instance, having taken successively a 'bus and two trains, and arrived in the neighbourhood of one of London's most depressing southern suburbs, he consented at last to explain matters.

'We go, Hastings, to see the one man in England who knows most of the underground life of China.'

'Indeed? Who is he?'

'A man you have never heard of—a Mr John Ingles. To all intents and purposes, he is a retired Civil Servant of mediocre intellect with a house full of Chinese curios with which he bores his friends and acquaintances. Nevertheless. I am assured by those who should know that the only man capable of giving me the information I seek is this same John Ingles.'

A few moments more saw us ascending the steps of

The Laurels, as Mr Ingles' residence was called. Personally I did not notice a laurel bush of any kind, so deduced that it had been named according to the usual obscure nomenclature of the suburbs.

We were admitted by an impassive-faced Chinese servant and ushered into the presence of his master. Mr Ingles was a squarely built man, somewhat yellow of countenance, with deep-set eyes that were oddly reflective in character. He rose to greet us, setting aside an open letter which he had held in his hand. He referred to it after his greeting.

'Sit down, won't you? Halsey tells me that you want some information and that I may be useful to you in the matter.'

'That is so, Monsieur. I ask of you if you have any knowledge of a man named Li Chang Yen.'

'That's rum—very rum indeed. How did you come to hear about the man?'

'You know him, then?'

'I've met him once. And I know something of him—not quite as much as I should like to. But it surprises me that anyone else in England should even have heard of him. He's a great man in his way—mandarin class and all that, you know—but that's not the crux of the matter. There's good reason to suppose that he's the man behind it all.'

'Behind what?'

'Everything. The Republic, the various upheavals of China, all this last unrest. It's even suspected that he was at the bottom of the Russian trouble. Wherever you find the hand of China, there you will find Li Chang Yen behind it. What's his game? Nobody knows—but you can be sure of this, it's deep, and it's Oriental. That man is the controlling brain of the East today. We don't understand the East—we never shall; but Li Chang Yen is its moving spirit. Not that he comes out into the lime-light—oh, not at all; never moves from his palace in Pekin. But he pulls strings—that's it, pulls strings—and things happen far away.'

'We have reason to believe that that is true,' Poirot quietly.

'Very odd, your knowing about him. Didn't fancy a soul in England had ever heard of him. I'd rather like to know how you did come to hear of him—if it's not indiscreet.'

'Not in the least, Monsieur. A man took refuge in my rooms. He was suffering badly from shock, but he managed to tell us enough to interest us in this Li Chang Yen. He described four people—the Big Four—an organisation hitherto undreamed of. No. 1 is Li Chang Yen, No. 2 is an unknown American, No. 3 an equally unknown French-woman, No. 4 may be called the executive of the organisa-tion—*the destroyer*. My informant died. Tell me, Monsieur, is that phrase known to you at all? The Big Four.'

'Not in connection with Li Chang Yen. No, I can't say it is. But I've heard it, or read it, just lately—and in some unusual connection too. Ah, I've got it.'

He rose and went across to an inlaid lacquer cabi-net—an exquisite thing, as even I could see. He returned with a letter in his hand.

'Here you are. Note from an old seafaring man I ran against once in Shanghai. Hoary old reprobate—maud-lin with drink by now, I should say. I took this to be the ravings of alcoholism.'

He read it aloud—

'Dear Sir,—You may not remember me, but you did me a good turn once in Shanghai. Do me another now. I must have money to get out of the country. I'm well hid here, I hope, but any day they may get me. The Big Four, I mean. It's life or death. I've plenty of money, but I daren't get at it, for fear of putting them wise. Send me a couple of hundred in notes. I'll repay it faithful—I swear to that.—Your servant, Sir,

  'Jonathan Whalley.

'Dated from Granite Bungalow, Hoppator, Dartmoor. I'm afraid I regarded it as rather a crude method of relieving me of a couple of hundred which I can ill spare. If it's any use to you—' He held it out.

'*Je vous remercie, Monsieur.* I start for Hoppator *à l'heure même.*'

'Dear me, this is very interesting. Supposing I came along too? Any objection?'

'I should be charmed to have your company, but we must start at once. We shall not reach Dartmoor until close on nightfall, as it is.'

John Ingles did not delay us more than a couple of minutes, and soon we were in the train moving out of Paddington bound for the West Country. Hoppator was a small village clustering in a hollow right on the fringe of the moorland. It was reached by a nine-mile drive from Moretonhamstead. It was about eight o'clock when we arrived; but as the month was July, the daylight was still abundant.

We drove into the village, and asked for the whereabouts of Granite Bungalow. A dozen willing hands pointed it out—a small grey cottage right in the centre of the village.

'There be t'Bungalow. Do yee want to see t'Inspector? A shocking murder t'was, seemingly. Pools of blood, they do say.'

We wasted no time in seeking out Inspector Meadows. Poirot introduced the magic name of Inspector Japp, and all was made easy for us.

'Yes, Sir; murdered this morning. A shocking business. They 'phoned to Moreton, and I came out at once. Looked a mysterious thing to begin with. The old man—he was about seventy you know and fond of his glass, from all I hear—was lying on the floor of the living-room. There was a bruise on his head, and his throat was cut from ear to ear. Blood all over the place, as you can understand. The woman who cooks for him, Betsy Andrews, she told us that her master had several little Chinese jade figures, that he'd told her were very valuable, and these had disappeared. That, of course, looked like assault and robbery; but there were all sorts of difficulties in the way of that solution. The old fellow had two people in the house: Betsy Andrews, who is a Hoppator woman; and a rough kind of man-servant, Robert Grant. Grant had gone to the farm to fetch the milk, which he does every day, and Betsy had stepped out to have a chat with a neighbour. She was only away twenty minutes—between ten and half-past—and the crime must have been done then. Grant returned to the house first. He went in by the back door, which was open—no one locks up doors round here; not in broad daylight, at

215

all events—put the milk in the larder, and went into his own room to read the paper and have a smoke. Had no idea anything unusual had occurred—at least, that's what *he* says. Then Betsy comes in, goes into the living-room, sees what's happened, and lets out a screech to wake the dead. That's all fair and square. Someone got in whilst those two were out, and did the poor old man in. But it struck me at once that he must be a pretty cool customer. He'd have to come right up the village street, or creep through someone's back yard. Granite Bungalow has got houses all round it, as you can see. How was it that no one had seen him?'

The Inspector paused with a flourish.

'Aha, I perceive your point,' said Poirot. 'To continue?'

'Well, Sir, fishy, I said to myself—fishy. And I began to look about me. Those jade figures, now. Would a common tramp ever suspect that they were valuable? Anyway, it was madness to try such a thing in broad daylight. Suppose the old man had yelled for help?'

'I suppose, Inspector,' said Mr Ingles, 'that the bruise, on the head was inflicted before death?'

'Quite right, Sir. First knocked him silly, the murderer did, and then cut his throat. That's clear enough. But how the dickens did he come or go? They notice strangers quick enough in a little place like this. It came to me all at once—nobody did come. I took a good look round. It had rained the night before, and there were footprints clear enough going in and out of the kitchen. In the living-room, there were two sets of footprints only (Betsy Andrews' stopped at the door)— Mr Whalley's (he was wearing carpet slippers) and another man's. The other man had stepped in the

216

bloodstains, and I traced his bloody footprints—I beg your pardon, Sir.'

'Not at all,' said Mr Ingles, with a faint smile; 'the adjective is perfectly understood.'

'I traced 'em to the kitchen—but not beyond. Point Number One. On the lintel of Robert Grant's door was a faint smear—a smear of blood. That's Point Number Two. Point Number Three was when I got hold of Grant's boots—which he had taken off—and fitted them to the marks. That settled it. It was an inside job. I warned Grant and took him into custody; and what do you think I found packed away in his portmanteau? The little jade figures and a ticket-of-leave. Robert Grant was also Abraham Biggs, convicted for felony and housebreaking five years ago.'

The Inspector paused triumphantly.

'What do you think of that, gentlemen?'

'I think,' said Poirot, 'that it appears to be a very clear case—an almost singularly clear case, if I may say so. This Biggs, or Grant, must be a very foolish and uneducated man.

'Oh, he is that—a rough, common sort of fellow. No idea of what a footprint may mean.'

'Clearly not a reader of detective fiction! Well, Inspector, I congratulate you. Any chance of our seeing the scene of the crime?'

'I'll take you there myself this minute. I'd like you to see those footprints.'

'I, too, should like to see them. Yes, yes, very interesting, very ingenious.'

We set out forthwith. Mr Ingles and the Inspector forged ahead. I drew Poirot back a little so as to be able to speak to him out of the Inspector's hearing.

'What do you really think, Poirot. Is there more in this than meets the eye?'

'That is just the question, *mon ami*. Whalley says plainly enough in his letter that the Big Four are on his track, and we know from our own experience that the Big Four is no chimera of the imagination. Yet everything seems to point to the fact that this man Grant committed the crime. Why did he do so? For the sake of the little jade figures? Or is he an agent of the Big Four? I confess that the whole thing seems more credible on the latter hypothesis. However valuable the jade, a man of that class was not likely to realise the fact—at any rate, not to the point of committing murder for them. (That, *par exemple*, ought to have struck the Inspector.) He could have stolen the jade and made off with it instead of committing a brutal and quite purposeless murder. Ah, yes; I fear our Devonshire friend has not used his little grey cells. He has measured footprints and omitted to reflect and arrange his ideas with the necessary order and method.'

The Inspector drew a key from his pocket and unlocked the door of Granite Bungalow. The day had been fine and dry, so our feet were not likely to leave any prints; nevertheless, we wiped them carefully on the mat before entering.

A woman came up out of the gloom and spoke to the Inspector, and he turned aside. Then he spoke over his shoulder.

'Have a good look round, Mr Poirot, and see all there is to see. I'll be back in about five minutes. By the way, here's Grant's boot. I brought it along with me for you to compare the impressions.'

218

We went into the living-room, and the sound of the Inspector's footsteps died away outside. Ingles was attracted immediately by some Chinese curios on a table in the corner, and went over to examine them. He seemed to take no interest in Poirot's doings. I, on the other hand, watched him with breathless interest. The floor was covered with a dark-green linoleum which was ideal for showing up footprints. A door at the farther end led into the small kitchen. From there another door led into the scullery (where the back door was situated), and another into the bedroom which had been occupied by Robert Grant. Having explored the ground, Poirot commented upon it in a low, running monologue.

'Here is where the body lay; that big, dark stain and the splashes all around mark the spot. Traces of carpet slippers and "number nine" boots, you observe, but all very confused. Then two sets of tracks leading to and from the kitchen: whoever the murderer was, he came in that way. You have the boot, Hastings? Give it to me.' He compared it carefully with the prints. 'Yes, both made by the same man, Robert Grant. He came in that way, killed the old man, and went back to the kitchen. He had stepped in the blood: see the stains he left as he went out? Nothing to be seen in the kitchen—all the village has been walking about in it. He went into his own room—no, first he went back again to the scene of the crime—was that to get the little jade figures? Or had he forgotten something that might incriminate him?'

'Perhaps he killed the old man the second time he went in?' I suggested.

'*Mais non*, you do not observe. On one of the outgoing footmarks stained with blood there is superimposed

219

an ingoing one. I wonder what he went back for—the little jade figures as an after-thought? It is all ridiculous—stupid.'

'Well, he's given himself away pretty hopelessly.'

'*N'est-ce pas?* I tell you, Hastings, it goes against reason. It offends my little grey cells. Let us go into his bedroom—ah, yes; there is the smear of blood on the lintel and just a trace of footmarks—blood-stained. Robert Grant's footmarks, and his only, near the body— Robert Grant the only man who went near the house. Yes, it must be so.'

'What about the old woman?' I said suddenly. 'She was in the house alone after Grant had gone for the milk. She might have killed him and then gone out. Her feet would leave no prints if she hadn't been outside.'

'Very good, Hastings; I wondered whether that hypothesis would occur to you. I had already thought of it and rejected it. Betsy Andrews is a local woman, well known hereabouts. She can have no connection with the Big Four; and, besides, old Whalley was a powerful fellow, by all accounts. This is a man's work—not a woman's.'

'I suppose the Big Four couldn't have had some diabolical contrivance concealed in the ceiling—something which descended automatically and cut the old man's throat and was afterwards drawn up again?'

'Like Jacob's ladder? I know, Hastings, that you have an imagination of the most fertile—but I implore of you to keep it within bounds.'

I subsided, abashed. Poirot continued to wander about, poking into rooms and cupboards with a profoundly dissatisfied expression on his face. Suddenly he uttered an excited yelp, reminiscent of a Pomeranian dog. I rushed to join him. He was standing in the larder in a dramatic attitude. In his hand he was brandishing a leg of mutton!

'My dear Poirot!' I cried. 'What is the matter? Have you suddenly gone mad?'

'Regard, I pray you, this mutton. But regard it closely!'

I regarded it as closely as I could, but could see nothing unusual about it. It seemed to me a very ordinary leg of mutton. I said as much. Poirot threw me a withering glance.

'But do you not see this—and this—and this—?'

He illustrated each 'this' with a jab at the unoffending joint, dislodging small icicles as he did so.

Poirot had just accused me of being imaginative, but I now felt that he was far more wildly so than I had ever been. Did he seriously think these slivers of ice were crystals of a deadly poison? That was the only construction I could put upon his extraordinary agitation.

'It's frozen meat,' I explained gently. 'Imported, you know. New Zealand.'

He stared at me for a moment or two and then broke into a strange laugh.

'How marvellous is my friend Hastings! He knows everything—but everything! How do they say—Inquire Within Upon Everything. That is my friend Hastings.'

He flung down the leg of mutton on to its dish again and left the larder. Then he looked through the window.

'Here comes our friend the Inspector. It is well. I have seen all I want to see here.' He drummed on the table absent-mindedly, as though absorbed in calculation, and then asked suddenly, 'What is the day of the week, *mon ami*?'

'Monday,' I said, rather astonished. 'What—?'

'Ah! Monday, is it? A bad day of the week. To commit a murder on a Monday is a mistake.'

Passing back to the living-room, he tapped the glass on the wall and glanced at the thermometer.

'Set fair, and seventy degrees Fahrenheit. An orthodox English summer's day.'

Ingles was still examining various pieces of Chinese pottery.

'You do not take much interest in this inquiry, Monsieur?' said Poirot.

The other gave a slow smile.

'It's not my job, you see. I'm a connoisseur of some things, but not of this. So I just stand back and keep out of the way. I've learnt patience in the East.'

The Inspector came bustling in, apologising for having been so long away. He insisted on taking us over most of the ground again, but finally we got away.

'I must appreciate your thousand politenesses, Inspector,' said Poirot, as we were walking down the village street again. 'There is just one more request I should like to put to you.'

'You want to see the body, perhaps, Sir?'

'Oh, dear me, no! I have not the least interest in the body. I want to see Robert Grant.'

'You'll have to drive back with me to Moreton to see him, Sir.'

'Very well, I will do so. But I must see him and be able to speak to him alone.'

The Inspector caressed his upper lip.

'Well, I don't know about that, Sir.'

'I assure you that if you can get through to Scotland Yard you will receive full authority.'

'I've heard of you, of course, Sir, and I know you've done us a good turn now and again. But it's very irregular.'

'Nevertheless it is necessary,' said Poirot calmly. 'It is necessary for this reason—Grant is not the murderer.'

'What? Who is, then?'

'The murderer was, I should fancy, a youngish man. He drove up to Granite Bungalow in a trap, which he left outside. He went in, committed the murder, came out, and drove away again. He was bare-headed, and his clothing was slightly blood-stained.'

'But—but the whole village would have seen him!'

'Not under certain circumstances.'

'Not if it was dark, perhaps; but the crime was committed in broad daylight.'

Poirot merely smiled.

'And the horse and trap, Sir—how could you tell that? Any amount of wheeled vehicles have passed along outside. There's no marks of one in particular to be seen.'

'Not with the eyes of the body, perhaps; but with the eyes of the mind, yes.'

The Inspector touched his forehead significantly with a grin at me. I was utterly bewildered, but I had faith in Poirot. Further discussion ended in our all driving back to Moreton with the Inspector. Poirot and I were taken to Grant, but a constable was to be present during the interview. Poirot went straight to the point.

'Grant, I know you to be innocent of this crime. Relate to me in your own words exactly what happened.'

The prisoner was a man of medium height with a

somewhat unpleasing cast of features. He looked a gaol-bird if ever a man did.

'Honest to God, I never did it,' he whined. 'Someone put those little glass figures amongst my traps. It was a frame-up, that's what it was. I went straight to my rooms when I came in, like I said. I never knew a thing till Betsy screeched out. S'welp me, God, I didn't.'

Poirot rose.

'If you can't tell me the truth, that is the end of it.'

'But, guv'nor—'

'You *did* go into the room—you *did* know your master was dead; and you were just preparing to make a bolt of it when the good Betsy made her terrible discovery.'

The man stared at Poirot with a dropped jaw.

'Come now, is it not so? I tell you solemnly—on my word of honour—that to be frank now is your only chance.'

'I'll risk it,' said the man suddenly. 'It was just as you say. I came in, and went straight to the master—and there he was, dead on the floor and blood all round. Then I got the wind up proper. They'd ferret out my record, and for a certainty they'd say it was me as had done him in. My only thought was to get away—at once—before he was found—'

'And the jade figures?'

The man hesitated.

'You see—'

'You took them by a kind of reversion to instinct, as it were? You had heard your master say they were valuable, and you felt you might as well go the whole hog. That I understand. Now answer me this. Was it the second time that you went into the room that you took the figures?'

'I didn't go in a second time. Once was enough for me.'

'You are sure of that?'

'Absolutely certain.'

'Good. Now, when did you come out of prison?'

'Two months ago.'

'How did you obtain this job?'

'Through one of them Prisoners' Help Societies. Bloke met me when I came out.'

'What was he like?'

'Not exactly a parson, but looked like one. Soft black hat and an affected way of talking. Got a broken front tooth. Spectacled chap. Saunders, his name was. Said he hoped I was repentant, and that he'd find me a good post. I went to old Whalley on his recommendation.'

Poirot rose once more.

'I thank you. I know all now. Have patience.' He paused in the doorway and added: 'Saunders gave you a pair of boots, didn't he?'

Grant looked very astonished.

'Why, yes, he did. But how did you know?'

'It is my business to know things,' said Poirot gravely.

After a word or two to the Inspector, the three of us went to the White Hart and discussed eggs-and-bacon and Devonshire cider.

'Any elucidations yet?' asked Ingles with a smile.

'Yes, the case is clear enough now; but, see you, I shall have a good deal of difficulty in proving it. Whalley was killed by order of the Big Four—but not by Grant. A very clever man got Grant that post and deliberately planned to make him the scapegoat—an easy matter with Grant's prison record. He gave him a pair of boots, one of two duplicate pairs. The other he kept himself. It was all so simple. When Grant is out of the house, and Betsy is chatting in the village (which she probably did every day of her life), he drives up wearing the duplicate boots, enters the kitchen, goes through into the living-room, fells the old man with a blow and then cuts his throat. Then he returns to the kitchen, removes the boots, puts on another pair, and, carrying the first pair, goes out to his trap and drives off again.'

Ingles looked steadily at Poirot.

'There's a catch in it still. Why did nobody see him?'

'Ah! That is where the cleverness of Number Four— for it *was* Number Four, I am convinced—comes in. Everybody saw him—and yet nobody saw him. You see, he drove up in a butcher's cart!'

I uttered an exclamation.

'The leg of mutton?'

'Exactly, Hastings, the leg of mutton. Everybody swore that no one had been to Granite Bungalow that morning, but nevertheless I found in the larder a leg of mutton, still frozen. It was Monday, so the meat must have been delivered that morning; for if on Saturday, in this hot weather, it would not have remained frozen over Sunday. So someone *had* been to the Bungalow, and a man on whom a trace of blood here and there would attract no attention.'

'Damned ingenious!' cried Ingles approvingly.

'Yes, he is clever, Number Four.'

'As clever as Hercule Poirot?' I murmured.

My friend threw me a glance of dignified reproach.

'There are some jests that you should not permit yourself, Hastings,' he said sententiously. 'Have I not saved an innocent man from being sent to the gallows? That is enough for one day.'

226

# BIBLIOGRAPHY

Agatha Christie's short stories typically appeared first in magazines and then in her short story books, which tended to be different collections in the UK and the US. This list attempts to catalogue the first publication of each of the stories included in this collection, and gives alternative story titles when used.

## Introduction

Excerpted from *An Autobiography* (1977) © 1977 Agatha Christie Limited.

## The Plymouth Express

© 1923 Agatha Christie Limited. First published in the UK in *The Sketch* No. 1575, 4 April 1923 and was reprinted in *The Under Dog and Other Stories* (US, 1951) and *Poirot's Early Cases* (UK, 1974). The story's plot was later reworked as the novel *The Mystery of the Blue Train* (1928).

## The Unbreakable Alibi

© 1929 Agatha Christie Limited. First published in the UK in *Holly Leaves*, the annual Christmas edition of *Illustrated*

*Sporting and Dramatic News*, December 1928 and was reprinted in *Partners in Crime* (UK, 1929).

## The Case of the Missing Will

© 1923 Agatha Christie Limited. First published in the UK in *The Sketch* No. 1605, 31 October 1923 and in the US in *The Blue Book Magazine* Vol. 40, No. 3, January 1925 under the title 'The Missing Will'. It was reprinted in *Poirot Investigates* (UK, 1924).

## Ingots of Gold

© 1928 Agatha Christie Limited. First published in the UK in *The Royal Magazine* issue 352, February 1928 and in the US in *Detective Story Magazine* Vol. 102, No. 1, 16 June 1928 under the title 'The Solving Six and the Golden Grave'. The story was reprinted in *The Thirteen Problems* (UK, 1932).

## Double Sin

© 1928 Agatha Christie Limited. First published in the UK in the *Sunday Dispatch*, 23 September 1928, and was reprinted in *Double Sin and Other Stories* (US, 1961) and *Poirot's Early Cases* (UK, 1974).

## The Hound of Death

© 1933 Agatha Christie Limited. First published in the UK in *The Hound of Death and Other Stories* (1933) and in the US in *The Golden Ball and Other Stories* (1971).

## The Cornish Mystery

© 1923 Agatha Christie Limited. First published in the UK in *The Sketch* No. 1609, 28 November 1923 and was reprinted in *The Under Dog and Other Stories* (US, 1951) and *Poirot's Early Cases* (UK, 1974).

## The Regatta Mystery

© 1936 Agatha Christie Limited. First published as 'Poirot and the Regatta Mystery' in the USA in the *Chicago Tribune*, 3 May 1936, and then in *Strand Magazine*, June 1936. It first appeared in its current form in *The Regatta Mystery and Other Stories* (US, 1939).

## The Flock of Geryon

© 1940 Agatha Christie Limited. First published in the US in *This Week* magazine, 26 May 1940, under the title 'Weird Monster' and in the UK in the *Strand Magazine* Issue 596, August 1940. It was reprinted in *The Labours of Hercules* (US and UK, 1946).

## The Edge

© 1927 Agatha Christie Limited. First published in the UK in *Pearson's Magazine* Issue 374, February 1927 and reprinted in *While the Light Lasts* (UK, 1997).

## The Bloodstained Pavement

© 1928 Agatha Christie Limited. First published in the UK in *The Royal Magazine* Issue 353, March 1928 and in the

US in *Detective Story Magazine* Vol. 102, No. 1, 16 June 1928 under the title 'The Solving Six and the Golden Grave'. The story was reprinted in *The Thirteen Problems* (UK, 1932).

## The Adventure of the Dartmoor Bungalow

© 1916 Agatha Christie Limited. First published in the UK in *The Sketch* Issue 1615, 9 January 1924 and reprinted in *The Big Four (Detective Club Edition)* (UK, 2016). The story was adapted for novelisation by Christie, and forms chapters three and four of *The Big Four* (UK and US, 1927) with the titles 'We Hear More About Li Chang Yen' and 'The Importance of a Leg of Mutton'.